Simon Mundy was born in 1954. He tr
director. From 1977 on he wrote for Tl
Listener and The Independent (as well as many magazines) on
classical music and was a frequent broadcaster on BBC Radio 3 & 4.
His first book, a biography of Elgar, was published in 1980. In the
1990s he directed the National Campaign for the Arts, founded the
European Forum for Arts and Heritage (now Culture Action Europe)
and directed festivals in Scotland and the Netherlands. This century
he has worked as an adviser to the Council of Europe and UNESCO,
given many seminars on culture and conflict at King's College London
and started Creative Guild, the Association of Creative Professionals.
As a poet he has read all over the world. He lives in Mid Wales.

Also by Simon Mundy

Novels
Silent Movements
Seeking The Spoils (writing as James Eno)
Shadows On The Island (writing as James Eno)

Poetry
Letter To Carolina
By Fax To Alice Springs
After The Games
More For Helen Of Troy

Music
Elgar
Glazunov
Purcell
Tchaikovsky

Politics
Making It Home

Flagey
In Autumn

by

Simon Mundy

Illustrated by
Kate Milsom

HAY
PRESS

First published in 2015 by Hay Press,
an imprint of Present Arts Ltd., Wales
www.haypress.co.uk

A CIP catalogue record for this book is available from the
British Library.
ISBN: 978-0-9932202-0-3

Cover drawing and illustrations © Kate Milsom 2015
Set in Georgia and designed by C & C Design Ltd.
www.candc-design.com

Printed in the UK by Berforts Information Press, Stevenage and
King's Lynn

Für Elise
another bagatelle

For Sue,
something for the
weekend!

All best wishes,

[signature]

Prestejgne 2015

Progress

I

Starting Saturday

A Morning Of Encounters

Saskia looked up moodily from her first machiato of the morning. The volume of the Spanish chatter from the table two along was insufferable. It was Saturday and barely ten. Surely Spanish could happen quietly sometimes?

At home in The Hague everybody knew that Saturday mornings were gentle domestic affairs, the cafés piping soft music, even classical, not the violent metal sounds of the Friday night *borrel*, the after office end of week drinking. But here in Brussels, despite the Flemish proximity, the sensible Dutch way held no sway. She sighed, sipped and glared.

Patrice, leaning back against the Italian coffee gismo in a brief interlude between customers, spotted her look and grinned. Keep out of a girl's way in the morning, any girl, blonde or not, he thought to himself. No point in prodding wasp nests. He wondered what she was. Northern, obviously, not fat enough to be English. But neither was she one of those huge Dutch fortresses. Too pretty to be German. He'd go Danish. It would explain the gloom.

Catrina shuffled up to the bar, eyes down as she rootled through the shapeless shaggy Afgan bag dangling from her left shoulder. Purse hunting, mobile hunting, keys hunting – the bloody sport occupied her for at least two hours a day. Her last and unlamented boyfriend, Bruno the Tory computer nerd, had told her this. It hadn't been hugely funny when she had been in love with him. Now the fact that he had bothered to calculate it and then produce the result with all the smugness of a well fed cat just demonstrated how unutterably sad he was.

Such a loser. He had lost her.

She saw Patrice's grin as she looked up, purse triumphantly in hand, and her day brightened. Now here was what she was looking for. Dishevelled, yes, off hand, often, but drop dead dishy all the way. She thought, I'd never find that in Derby.

Across at the Spanish table, it sounded as if the momentary hilarity had been replaced by furious argument. All four people, three men, one women, were talking at once, the woman most volubly. In fact, Mercedes would have told anyone in perfect French or florid (though not always easy to catch) English, they were only discussing whether it was going to rain. This is usually a near certainty in Brussels, which is what Mercedes was trying to tell the boys – Jordi, Jose and his younger brother Joaquin, the latter only up from Valencia for a long weekend, hence the discussion. Should they risk going all the way out to Heysel and the park round the Atomium or should they just stick around Flagey, take in a film and then see which bar sounded good for the evening? But this – the shape and calibre of the clouds, the direction of the wind, what had happened last Saturday – all had to be examined with conviction or not at all.

In his turn Patrice caught the beam of Catrina's smile as he turned and half inclined his head to take her order. At least there was one happy customer this morning. This girl looked OK too, if in that disorganised way that all English girls had (he assumed she was English, even if she wasn't fat). It was as if they had got out of bed and failed to put the bits of their body together in the right order. Her hair, for example, an interesting sandy colour, but pulled tight at the back with wisps escaping instead of being allowed to flow full and free. And that baggy mauve T-shirt, a size too big, stuffed into a much too formal jacket for the weekend and completely hiding her figure, the rest of which (he noted appreciatively as he glanced at her jeans while she worked out the French for fresh mint tea) was surprisingly neat and trim without being skinny. And the bag, one of those Afghan woolly creations that reduced any woman to looking homeless.

Across by the window Saskia was aware that her sharpened glare was having absolutely no effect whatever on the Spanish contingent. She had neither seen, nor would have cared if she had, Patrice's amused interception. She sipped the machiato

3

and returned to her laptop screen where she was attempting to log into her Ziggie account – that world artery of intimate friendship that made lives so much more public than previous generations would have thought bearable. Even this, though, was beginning to torment her. The wireless system in the café was so slow that it had already taken her fifteen minutes – almost the whole machiato – just to get her to the password stage but then Ziggie wouldn't let her in because by the time the signal had been sent, the system had given up waiting and just demanded the password again.

Behind the bar Patrice pulled a handful of mint leaves from a plastic box, shoved them in a glass, poured on the hot water and added a long spoon, sugar and tiny slab of chocolate to a saucer. Catrina watched him dreamily, massaging the Euro coins between her fingers as if they were his hair. He wound a paper napkin round the glass and tucked it in place with a practised twist. Catrina could barely bring herself to pay but then thought that if she gave him the coins instead of putting them on the bar her fingers might meet his. They did, for an instant and she tingled. If Patrice tingled, though, he didn't show it; merely chucked out a 'merci' and moved briskly to the till.

Catrina adjusted the bag on her shoulder, picked up her tea, turned and looked around for a table. There was a small one free, two in from the window, between a woman working at a computer and a jolly group chatting away in what she could tell even from the bar was Spanish. She began a slow walk over, her eyes firmly on the lip of the glass so as not to spill.

Jose was adamant, and determined that Mercedes would not pen them all inside all day just because it might rain. They would go to Heysel. Mercedes was not so easily defeated, however, and wailed to Jordi for support.

For Saskia, just as Ziggie blocked her entrance once again, the wail from Mercedes was too much. She grabbed her coffee cup, pushed back the chair with determination and stepped forward. There was a word to be had and it should be comprehensible in any language.

Shut up.

It was unfortunate that Saskia and Catrina should arrive at the same side of the spare table at the same time, one intent on making her point, the other equally intent on making it to the table. As Saskia strode forward she nudged Catrina's bag hard. The bag lurched from the shoulder and slipped heavily down the elbow. Mint tea was catapulted upwards and when it came down – glass and extras first, the leaves, then boiling water – it fell into the moving bag and over the black silk shirt on Mercedes' back.

The wail became a shriek. Catrina howled. The boys jumped up. Patrice spun round.

Typical, thought Saskia. She was not going to take the blame for their foolishness. Taking the blame was not her way. If that stupid girl had been looking where she was going and if those Spanish idiots had not been shouting like children, nothing would have happened. Without a word she went back to her table and began to shut down her computer.

Jordi was livid. It was clear Mercedes was in a deal of pain from her scalded back and that great oaf of a woman had not said a word of apology. While Patrice emerged from the bar with a cloth soaked in cold water, Jordi pushed past the lamenting Catrina to confront the Dutchwoman.

'You pain her,' he accused in halting English, 'you will make sorry.'

Saskia shrugged. 'Why?'

Jordi was staggered. 'Why?' he repeated.

'You make too much noise. She gets hurt. It's right.'

Jordi Santal was a Catalan gentleman and hitting girls was against every code in his twenty-six year old book but this was provocation beyond his belief. How could someone cause another to have shocking burns and not show even a scintilla of regret? Patrice began to pad down Mercedes' shirt with the cool cloth as Catrina stood by miserable and helpless. Out of the corner of his eye he saw Jordi straighten threateningly. Saskia hadn't noticed. She was calmly packing away her computer.

Patrice gestured to Joaquin to take over the care of Mercedes, handed over the cloth, and moved swiftly to Jordi's side. He laid a hand on the Catalan's arm.

'Non Monsieur.'

Jordi glared at him, then relaxed.

'Madame,' Patrice began in French to Saskia, then switched to English, 'you were at fault I believe. Now you will apologise, if you please.'

It was not a notion in Saskia's constitution. She looked up at both men and regarded them with contempt.

'I will not,' she said simply.

'Then you will leave,' stated Patrice.

'I am leaving.'

'And you will not come back. Again. Jamais.'

Saskia looked up in astonishment. 'You ban me?'

'Oui, Madame. You are banned.'

The Dutch girl looked around the Café Franck. She was bemused. Nobody had ever banned her from anything, nor thrown her out. She stood still waiting for things to change, to return to normal, for a usual Saturday routine of two machiatos and Ziggie to reassert itself.

'Maintenant, Madame' insisted Patrice, 'out. Please.' And he moved to open the door to her right. In silence Saskia obeyed.

Outside, the first drops of rain began to fall.

~~~

Fidel Looks Up

Fidel sat in his wonted corner of the Café Franck in Flagey and perused the Saturday essay columns of Le Matin. It seemed that somebody had translated one of Paul Scheffer's Amsterdam contributions to Volkskrant in which that tousled haired pedagogue was arguing that the age of cosmopolitanism was over and only local politics mattered any more. Fidel sniffed, muttered 'troublemaker', and frowned.

Despite his name, Fidel was not Cuban or even Iberian of any stock. To the world, his publisher and his new students he was Guus van der Looy, Professor of Applied Rhetoric at the Free University of Ixelles. And despite that deeply Flemish name, he was Francophone in language, attitude, lecturing style and habit. He always wore black or grey, never wore a tie, and if the aforementioned Paul Scheffer's hair was tousled up in Amsterdam, Professor van der Looy's was a storm of white, a carefully encouraged Medusa's head of independent anarchy.

The name thing had developed years earlier when a couple of students from St. Andrews, having a little Scottish difficulty with the version of his name in English, had rendered it as 'on the loo' with predictable results: laughter at a particularly inappropriate section of his lecture on Cicero. Unable to mention him without sniggers and giggles, they had shortened it to VDL, which wasn't much better. Fidel had been the agreed outcome. After all, what could be a more fitting name for a Franco-Flemish anarchist of unwavering gravity and interminable intellectual flow? It had stuck, not just for the Scottish but for all; students and staff alike. At first its owner had hated it but as the years went by he took to enjoying it with the same affection as its begetters had intended.

This Saturday morning Fidel was not at his most amiable, however. More than sufficient ten year-old Rioja had slipped into the system on Friday night, largely because the jazz concert he had dragged himself to in a depressing concrete theatre in one of the side streets off the square had turned out to be 'new fusion', in other words not jazz but rock music with an occasional saxophone. It was not that he didn't enjoy rock music. He had cut his intellectual teeth in the seventies, after all. It was mucking up jazz that he objected to. Fidel had fled to the bar, where he found the Rioja was better than to be expected out of plastic glasses.

Normally one glass to douse his grumble would have been enough before he clambered home up the hill but also taking a break from the noise was the scarfed and silent figure of Hugo de Greef, once incumbent of the substantial director's office of the performance complex of which Café Franck was a merely a corner. De Greef was the perfect foil for a grumble, partly because he never said much and partly because he couldn't care less. He listened, finished his drink, and wandered back into the hall with a noncommittal nod, leaving Fidel alone with the wisp of a barmaid who (he discovered somewhere about glass three) was called Elise and just starting a postgraduate degree in Modern Circus Studies (MCS, she called it before explaining patiently). Fidel was still not sure he quite grasped what modern circus studies entailed but by Elise he was enthralled until swamped by the audience when the music stopped.

The swamping had been the excuse for several more glasses, of course, as the many who knew Fidel assumed he had been with them in the theatre throughout and sought his opinion. He was, after all, an opinion former, a man of whom it had once been said on Brussels TV that to be of lasting fame in the city one had to have been pronounced significant by Guus van der Looy. He pronounced, drank and, after a slightly unprofessorial farewell to Elise, was respectfully escorted to his door by three of last year's graduates.

By the time on Saturday morning when Mercedes was goading Saskia into action, Fidel was wishing the music had stopped a little earlier up the bottle. Had Elise offered to show him all the moves that went with contemporary trapeze, as long as he tried a freshener with his coffee, he was certain his refusal would have been profoundly firm.

He watched in glum disapproval as the drama unfolded – the collision with Catrina, the scalding of Mercedes and the ousting of Saskia. It was not what Café Franck was for at breakfast time.

Even from his regular corner by the most distant window the fuss was loud and unsettling. The café chatter diminished to a whisper, all quiet except for the relentless piped music. The wailing of Mercedes, the remonstrations of Jordi and Jose, and most of all the purposeful arrival of Patrice from behind the bar, was enough to interrupt even the most earnest of morning conversations.

From the kitchen the pot-washers emerged, drying their hands on ankle-length aprons. There were three of them, two of whom Fidel knew all too well and disregarded as being perfectly fitted to their role and unlikely to rise above the ordinary, whatever their nominal field of study. They had served him drinks, they had swabbed his table, and they had treated him with about the same interest as any of the one-time drinkers who found their way to the Café Franck before a show next door. But the third of them was new and different; so slight and fragile she barely filled the jeans that tried to support her apron, her long black hair massed on top of her head in the current Flagey fashion.

Fidel's hung-over heart had a little skip. Elise.

Her back was to Fidel but he had watched enough of it the night before – indeed talked to it for many minutes at a time – to be utterly certain. Why the flutter of pleasure, he wondered? Surely he was beyond such things and the entrancement had been just from the Rioja and the accident of his lone drinking as the 'new fusion' blared. Apparently not.

As the door closed behind the humiliated Saskia and the normal café buzz resumed, Elise turned to go back to the kitchen. She saw Fidel, caught his eye and smiled.

Fidel smiled back, nodded and resumed his scan of the paper. Le Matin was no longer engrossing. The pain behind his eyes was unaccountably lifting.

~~~

Catrina Mulls

Soon after Saskia, the errant Dutchwoman, had been ejected from Café Franck (not so much for spilling boiling mint tea over Mercedes but more for refusing to admit it was her fault), the Spanish quartet left too. Mercedes was still sore and in some shock but the hot water had now turned cold and the damp blouse was sticking uncomfortably against her skin. As he rose after her, Jordi considerately draped his own jacket round her shoulders.

Catrina felt at a bit of a loss. Her morning had seemed all very straightforward ten minutes earlier. Now she couldn't decide whether to stay or leave too, whether somehow the fact that it was her tea that had been jolted over the Spanish girl's back made her guilty by association. She stood at the bar and looked around. Nobody seemed to be staring at her now the drama was finished. The place looked much as it had done. New people – people who had seen nothing – were coming in and lining up for Patrice's attention. Some nearby did glance at Catrina but only to find out whether she was being served. She rather wondered that herself.

The answer came swiftly and, like everything else that morning, seemed to have nothing to do with anything she had instigated. A new mint tea was placed in front of her on the bar and with it a glass – a flute. She looked up with a puzzled frown.

Patrice was grinning at her.

'You wanted a mint tea, no?' he asked in English.

'Yes, I did. Thank you. But...'

'Well there it is. And I feel you may be a little weak after our little incident.'

Catrina admitted that she was a touch wobbly.

'Ah, wobbly!' repeated Patrice with great solemnity. 'I thought so. And when one is wobbly I find champagne is the only thing. But it is early still, so for you a Kir Royale.'

'Are you sure? Isn't it expensive?'

Patrice shrugged, 'Not when it is from me,' he said reasonably. 'Where are you sitting?'

It was yet another issue that Catrina hadn't settled at all. She searched the room for solutions. The café was almost full by now. Her original table for two just behind her was now firmly occupied by a couple in their fifties.

'I don't know,' Catrina said lamely and felt it.

'No matter,' Patrice picked up her champagne flute with a flourish, 'you will sit at our table.'

Catrina found that 'our table' was the one at the end of the bar just by the food counter. It had a reserved sign firmly plonked in the middle and nobody had dared to disagree. Patrice placed the tea and aperitif so that Catrina would sit on the low bench that ran along the back wall but she preferred a more upright chair – she felt short and reaching up from the bench to the champagne had too many echoes of childhood and failing to touch the floor – so she moved one to the end of the table.

She watched Patrice as he slotted back behind the bar and whispered to one of the girls, pointing Catrina out. The girl nodded and passed the message along the line. Presumably the order was that the Englishwoman was accepted in the private enclave.

The Kir Royale was delicious; she sipped hesitantly as if Patrice was really joking and it was just blackcurrant and tonic water. The morning so far was becoming extraordinary.

Catrina had a flat, or a room with a rudimentary cubicle for a bathroom and a cooking space squeezed unhygenically into a void against its wall, a few hundred metres to the east, away from the fashionable side of the square, in the dingey streets that sat in the basin between Flagey and the viaduct carrying the railway from Leopold station. She had no idea who Alfred Giron was but clearly the Belgians didn't think much of him either, given the street they had named after him.

She had been in Brussels for three months, ever since finding a job as second (i.e. horribly paid) assistant to an MEP whose politics she loathed but who had advertised in her local paper just as her MA in European Studies had been completed and she wondered what the hell she was going to do with it. She was still wondering but this interval of Brussels semi-poverty was a way of postponing a decision until after her twenty-fourth birthday. The job was also a way of almost convincing her doubtful father in Derby, to whom only engineering was a real job, that she might one day be able to earn a living.

She had begun to adopt Café Franck as her Saturday morning hang-out only the week before, two days after being dumped for a fleshy Italian by the hooray Henry specimen who worked one tower in the Parliament away; a revolting creature (she now thought) called Bruno who had turned out to be even more Tory than her boss but who had seemed to offer the promised land in her first tentative weeks in the vast steel barns of European political chatter.

Freshly dumped, the last week had been salutary and lonely. She had come to the café that morning not just for the solace of mint tea and average music but to review her life. About the time the mint tea hit the floor that review was not reading too well. Now, champagne sweetened with blackcurrant at her lips and Patrice in her eye line, it was starting to shape up.

Ever the pessimist, Catrina wondered how long it could last.

In the corner behind her the customers were being politely shunted away and a dais set up for the late morning live music that was the café's Saturday special. There didn't seem to be too many big speakers or drum kits, she was happy to see as she shifted round: just keyboard, guitar and voice so far, by the look of it. Catrina relaxed and abandoned the hard chair, moving onto the comfortable padded bench so she could see better, even if she became nearly invisible herself. From there, though, she would have musicians to her left and the constantly moving vision of Patrice's bottom to her right. The cocktail was finished, she noted with a pang. She tried the cooling mint tea. Definitely not in the same class.

What were her prospects? Should she stay or should she go – not just in the Café Franck but in the European Parliament, in Brussels, in...? Only one thing was certain. To go back to Derby was the sort of slow death reserved for spinsters in a Victorian novel. Maybe she should go and volunteer in Malawi or somewhere, or Peru?

As the gloom descended and the indecision deepened Patrice appeared at the corner of the table, another Kir Royale in one hand and a beer in the other.

'So what shall I call you?' he asked, flopping onto the bench beside her.

~~~

An Unparliamentary Morning

It was a rare Saturday when Esko Nystrom was not required to fly back to Finland and be nice to Forward Party activists on the shores of the Baltic – or, to be exact, the Gulf of Bothnia. There had been invitations for this weekend but they had been merely his as adjuncts to his wife, a national politician famous (or notorious) in a way no European one ever was. It meant she was certainly too busy to see him, even if she had wanted to.

In theory he and his wife Rikka were perfect foils for each other. Esko was Swedish-speaking Finnish, forty-four, and seen to be at the peak of his career as a progressive politician on the centre left of his country's undemonstrative politics. Rikka, though, was twelve years younger and had the energy and conviction he seemed to lack in public. He had 'discovered' her just out of university graduate life six years earlier, 'mentored' her into the party, and then married her – at which point he was elected to Brussels and she to Helsinki and her career as the darling of the TV left consigned him to the status of also-ran. He was not sure he minded that but he did mind the feeling that she had not only outgrown his reputation but his adoration as well. Brussels at the weekend, at Café Franck – just across the lake from his first floor apartment – was as much a haven from his doubts as his duties.

Esko settled with a notebook and an espresso, chased with the first beer of the day, at an unexceptional table round the L of the bar's geography from the musicians. He was not to know it but by that simple action he incurred the silent fury of Fidel whose constant sight of Elise, patrolling her side of the bar beyond Patrice, was promptly compromised. It was possible to shift, lean and peer around the Finn's wide back but not without looking either desperate or drunk. Fidel was conscious of the fact that he was in danger of leering as it was. The only thing to do was hold his ground and hope that the large lump would soon melt away.

He didn't and, even if he had been aware of Fidel's eyes trying to make him transparent, he would not have moved. There were very few tables for the single person still vacant now that the music was beginning.

Esko tossed back the coffee, slaked his mouth with beer and contemplated the blank pages of his notebook. Bringing it had been a reflex. He was determined to avoid the reports, urgent messages, party policy documents and general parliamentary detritus that filled his laptop and phone screen on this first day of his free weekend. Those he would tackle on Sunday in the flat, when their relevance would be both more imminent and less daunting with a CD of Mendelssohn string quartets to soften the process. But he found doing nothing with his eyes and hands a virtual impossibility so something had to be done, otherwise he would stare and fiddle and fidget until the point of coming to the café to wind down was utterly lost.

Making a work list was just as pointless. He had long been pressured to set out his political philosophy in a long essay but that was for a late night with the computer. What did one put in a notebook? He left it on the table with a pen as he went to the bar for more beer and coffee, alienating Fidel even further as he was granted the same warming smile from Elise that the professor had thought special to him.

Esko took in the glory of the smile but whereas for Fidel it had opened new vistas of potential adoration, for Esko it just made him feel homesick and lonely. Suddenly the calm solitude of his free Saturday was chipped. Instead of the reality of life in Vaasa – the indifference of Rikka, the rush, the long journey and constant airports – he thought of a lazy morning in bed with her as it had been only four short years before. Back at the table he suddenly knew what the notebook was for. He would write her a love letter.

With his usual neatness Esko hung his jacket over the back of the chair, set his coffee cup and beer glass at the perfect oblique angle, and opened the notebook at its virgin first page. This would just be a draft, he told himself, so there was no point in starting with Rikka's name. He would just start saying what needed to be said.

The music was beginning, first a few chords to test the

sound system, then the ice-breaker number, vigorous and fresh. Round the other side of the bar Catrina was halfway down her second Kir Royale, tapping her foot and making sure Patrice bumped against her knee. Behind Esko, a defeated Fidel was grumpily putting on his black coat.

Esko was oblivious. He stared out across the square, the lake, to the building where he lived. He tried to compose. He wrote absently.

Somewhere towards the middle of the band's third song he looked down at the page, hoping there might be sense.

'Rikka, Rikka, Rikka, Rikka....' was all he had managed, covering a page. His eyes clouded with tears.

'Esko? Esko, are you OK?'

The Parliamentarian looked up, bemused for a moment. Then he took a swig of beer and pulled himself up straight. Standing over him was his Parliamentary assistant Mariana.

'Fine,' he managed half a smile. 'Fine. Sit down.'

~~~

Uncalled-for Assistance

Mariana was confused. Firstly she was confused to see her employer sitting in Café Frank on a Saturday morning when he would normally have been in Finland, secondly she was confused by the look on Esko's face of desperate and distant pain. He was looking at her as if she was a complete stranger. Maybe it was not Esko at all. Maybe the Member of the European Parliament was employing a double so that he could be somewhere else entirely.

'Esko?' she asked tentatively, pausing as she unwrapped her scarf.

He took a moment to respond, studying her face. She frowned. Gradually his eyes seemed to link back to his mind.

'Oh, Mariana. I'm sorry. I was thinking too hard.' Mariana noticed that he closed a notebook hurriedly as he spoke. 'What are you doing here?'

She shrugged. 'Same as you.'

Esko smiled as if he doubted it. 'Are you meeting somebody? Or would you like to join me?' He was hoping she would say no, he realised. It had been an instinctive invitation but he really did not want to discuss work, politics or the state of the world that morning. Neither did he want to spend too much time alone with the junior and more neurotic of his two assistants (though the other, a man, seemed to be permanently off sick). She was a young party enthusiast, just as Rikka had been at the same age, and though he was happy to have her around the office, this morning she was a combination of reminder, distraction and warning that he was finding immediately difficult.

She smiled back, pulled out the spare chair and sat,

unravelling the multicoloured scarf that seemed to be unending. 'Thanks, I'd love too. I'm not seeing anyone till later, I mean...' she wondered whether she had somehow disappointed him, 'I can stay as long as you like. I often come in for the music. I like it here.'

'So do I. Somehow all the noise makes it very peaceful.'

'Peaceful?' Mariana's confusion extended.

'Yes. I don't have to notice other people. There is too much noise to hear their conversations and too many to draw attention to themselves.'

'I see,' said Mariana, but didn't.

'Can I get you a coffee, or a drink?'

'Yes, please. Oh, no – not yet. I need to smoke first.' She began to wind up the scarf she had just unwound far enough to leave only one revolution round her neck.

'Well, when you are ready, what would you like?' Esko asked, relaxing at the thought that he would have a few moments of solitude left so that he could banish the pointless dreams of Rikka. 'I'll have it waiting for you by the time you've finished.'

Mariana was standing again. 'Not coffee,' she admitted, 'I have that all week. Would a glass of rosé be too much?'

'Not at all,' said Esko. If anything it was probably cheaper than the coffee, he thought.

He watched Mariana walk out through the door and reappear lighting a cigarette on the other side of the window before making any movement himself. The smile faded from his face as he looked down at the notebook, opened its cover, and saw the pathetic scrawls of Rikka's name. Was she just too busy with her own rise to fame and glory to have time for him, he wondered, or was she really being a calculating bitch who now had better fish to fry?

Esko waited until he could see Mariana had half finished her fag before going to the bar and asking Elise for her wine, and another beer for himself. As he turned back to the table, he nearly collided with a woman, Catrina, who was walking behind him on the way to the underground toilet.

'So sorry,' she said in English, 'that seems to be happening all the time to me today.' Esko returned her wan smile and sat down, just as Mariana pushed through the curtains and joined him to claim her wine. He wondered what on earth they were going to talk about.

'I thought you would be in Finland?' she began.

'No need. And besides, two days here with no office to go to is as good as a rest.'

His assistant's brow furrowed, 'But didn't we refuse an invitation from Moldova because you are too busy?'

'Possibly – and I am: for Moldova.'

Mariana look troubled. 'Isn't it important?'

'No.'

She sipped her very small glass of wine, served in a thick water glass, the café's way of showing it only approved of beer.

Esko could see that her estimation of him was slipping. She was serious about everything, he realised, and it probably didn't matter whether it was the future of Moldova or the yellow bellied Amazon tree frog, she expected him, as an MEP, to rush out and save it. Suddenly he was very tired of earnest young women. Mariana was staring at her glass, perhaps trying to come up with another starting line for the conversation. He wasn't going to help her. He had come to Café Franck for a solitary morning drink and he would have it on his own terms, whether it alienated her or not. The music was edging up in volume anyway, cutting out the need for constant talk.

Catrina climbed the narrow stairs into the café from the toilet and started on her way back to her new privileged position at the staff table. She was feeling nicely tipsy, just enough of a champagne high to make the world feel a wonderful place.

Then she spotted Mariana. They had seen each other a few times in the lift at the Parliament. Catrina was in a different office tower, she thought, one further from the political left, but once or twice they had shared a table in the level 3 bar – but then who hadn't? It was the place where most of Europe hung out when they couldn't face the computer or the committee meetings were too dull to be borne any longer. Mariana looked strained, Catrina thought. Perhaps the man she was with was giving her a hard time.

'Hi,' said Catrina, stopping by the table, her back to Esko, 'do you live round here?'

Mariana looked up and gradually recognised Catrina. 'Not

far,' she admitted, 'do you want to join us?'

'No thanks, I'm sitting up by the music already.' She looked Esko critically. Maybe the girl (she couldn't remember the name, if she had ever known it) needed rescuing, 'but you can come up there with me if you want.'

'Well...' Mariana looked nervously at Esko.

'You go on,' he said, trying desperately not to look relieved, 'you see enough of me all week.'

'If you're sure?'

'Sure.'

'Thanks.'

'Who's he?' asked Catrina with an edge as they turned he corner of the bar out of Esko's sight.

'My boss. Esko.'

'Creepy?'

'I don't think so.' Mariana was frowning, though, and trying to analyse the conversation as she sat down across from Catrina. He certainly had not done anything creepy. He had shown no interest in her whatever. Maybe she hated that. Maybe she didn't. A few minutes later, as Patrice folded her under the same wing as Catrina, she no longer cared. Yes, she did.

Catrina, though, read too much into the barman's welcome and was instantly depressed and jealous in equal measure. She decided to get drunk before lunch.

~~~

Change Of Habit

When Saskia was thrown out of Café Franck after the incident of the mint tea and Mercedes' back she stood for a moment outside and considered her options. It had begun to drizzle. She pulled her collar up and glanced round the square, wondering whether to forsake the scene of her humiliation for ever or whether to make her point by picking a rival establishment. She was Dutch, not Flemish, and so the protestant combination of stubbornness and self-denial held out. She would not renounce Place Flagey, even if one corner of it was barred to her.

Across the street the tram stop was rejected. Behind her, past the great 1930s block of the old television centre that had become the Flagey art house, there was a small jazz bar but it was a late night smoky haunt with hard high stools and canned music, not right for the start of an early autumn Saturday. Beside the tram stop there was the most traditional of the square's French cafés, cramped and serving average coffee and bad house wine (though better, it had to be admitted, than the Café Franck's). It was for regulars, though, especially middle aged men, or the occasional couple of girls wanting to gossip away from friends. It was not for tall blondes in a bad mood.

The other two options were on the furthest side – an indifferent and impersonal joint which showed TV sports, permanently tuned to the most obscure (and therefore with the cheapest subscription). Saskia had occasionally ventured in during evenings when she wanted a basic Belgian meal with no discussion and no frippery, but now she wanted somewhere less functional, that would take the sour memory of her ejection out of mind.

That left one final corner to explore: the Café Levantine. Saskia had never ventured there, assuming it to be yet another of the thousand kebab and coffee houses that furnished Brussels' miscellaneous Islamic communities with meagre jobs. This morning, though, she was angry enough with Belgian culture to risk it.

The centre of the café was dominated by a circular staircase. At one side was a bar with a sign through an opening to toilets and extra seating – a secluded backroom. In the main space tables were distributed round the walls but there were none in the main body of the room, as if it had been left empty for dancing. The tables themselves were intricate metal constructions, the tops filled in with decorative eastern tiles. Against the windows benches were set, upholstered lavishly with red velveteen and augmented by lines of cushions. The room was warm and smelled of spices and coffee. Soft modulated songs, heavy with slides and quartertones, piped from speakers high in the ceiling.

At approaching midday, Saskia was on her own. She stood in the middle of the room, thrown by unaccustomed indecision. To the right the tables seemed cold and distant and too open to the street. To the left all the benches had the window at their back. There were three, one hemmed in by the double door, one by the bar and one between the two. That would leave her prey to whoever sat down on either side, and she would be watched from the bar though, since there seemed to be nobody about, that might not be a problem. She opted for the least conspicuous table, in the corner furthest from the square, but which gave the vantage of the whole café with the exception of the bar itself.

Nobody had seen her come in and, as she found after ten minutes, sitting in her corner they were unlikely to unless some more noisy customers arrived.

Saskia debated whether to explore or just sit and wait for something to happen. The second course was against her nature but then so was seeking service in a place that should provide it. She had had enough of ordering from the bar, as at Café Franck. She wanted to be noticed – noticed and deferred to. She settled back against the cushions, thought about breaking the law by lighting a cigarette, resisted, and set her laptop on the table in front of her.

It was just firing up and trying to find a wireless signal when a procession of young men came in, all dressed in the familiar uniform of the immigrant streets, hooded tracksuits, baggy trousers and elaborate trainers. There were five of them, and they could have been from anywhere east or south of the Mediterranean in origin. Saskia, her own home town as much Moroccan and Surinamese in population as Dutch, watched them without curiosity as they passed through into the back room. They seemed to have ignored her entirely but something must have been said behind the scenes for a few seconds later a bustling man in his fifties hurried out and stood apologising to Saskia.

It was better than being thrown out, she decided, and ordered a coffee.

The man hovered. 'Normal or our Lebanese?'

Saskia concentrated. Be different, she thought, shake off the routine and the feel of the Café Franck. New start.

She opted for Lebanese and was rewarded by a warm wave of approval from her host.

'Do you like it sweet or medium?'

She had no idea but was not going to admit it. 'Medium,' she said, as though it was an automatic preference.

By the time the coffee arrived her computer had found a way online, a family and a loving couple had drifted in and two more boys had made their way to the back. The coffee was served with ceremony. On a beaten copper tray was placed the tiny cup, a candle burner and the little flask of steaming black sludge. That she expected. She had not expected the flask of water flavoured with violets, the saucers of cashews and sugared almonds, the scented washing dish for her fingers, or the hot napkin. For the first time all day Saskia smiled. She looked around the small room with new affection. Maybe she had found a new home.

II

Saturday Afternoon
And Evening

A Dithering

After three Kir Royales, and a couple of Baileys that Patrice had recommended to soak up the acid, Catrina was in tremendous form. The music coming from the nondescript trio to her left had taken on unsuspected elegance and profundity as she hummed and swayed, spurred on by the occasional stroke of her leg that Patrice gave it in the intervals between customers.

The Finnish girl Mariana, her distant colleague from the European Parliament's corps of young assistants, had disappeared for one of her many smokes in the chill drizzle outside and Catrina was not exactly missing her. In fact she was entirely oblivious of her; a fact that Mariana would have found as painful as it was incomprehensible.

Mariana was consumed by the thought that everybody was thinking about her, continuously and simultaneously, and that whenever she could be seen her body was a natural focus for attention. It was why she made sure she stayed as thin as possible; a dual reasoning – maybe she would be so thin nobody would see her but if they did, she would be irreproachable, an epitome of slender. If Mariana had a secret desire to vanish, like the smile on the Cheshire cat, she spoiled it by never sitting still and springing up every few minutes to find a smoking zone, which usually involved pacing up and down outside a window, drawing the gazes of those inside, for Mariana, her brown hair flowing beyond her shoulders, was a lovely girl. Few wanted to engage further, though. There was the hint of neurosis about the pacing, the extreme skinniness, the smoking, the penetrating eyes, the incongruous deep contralto voice, that spelled trouble for all who wanted a quiet life. Already this morning Esko and Catrina had done their best to slip out of her orbit, though the latter too late to succeed.

It was when the music stopped and Catrina made her second trip round the bar and down the steep stairs to the loos that he realised she was not quite as in control as she had assumed. Descending required concentration which seemed to be in short supply. Re-emerging into the daylight had its challenges too. Catrina wondered for a moment whether this vague shock and disorientation was how a new butterfly felt. She did a little twirl to explore the idea and nearly repeated her tea tossing exploit of earlier in the day but caught the edge of the bar before catastrophe struck.

She giggled perhaps a touch louder than she had intended

as she skipped back to her seat. Patrice watched as he finished pouring a beer and smiled. Things were going nicely.

Catrina flopped back onto the bench and looked around the room with a sudden finality. She really should go home. The music had stopped. Her glasses were empty. Talking to Mariana again when she came back would be a chore too far.

Patrice was pulling a beer with one hand while scraping the froth from a full glass with the other and the English distrust of instant emotions bubbled to the surface as Catrina watched him twist and serve with brisk efficiency. He had taken advantage – kindly, she admitted – but it must all be a front. She looked down at her unpretentious clothes with doubt, her stubby knees, her indistinct bosom. The drinks meant nothing, the hand on her leg even less. She desired him, that was clear and he had sensed it. He wanted diversion on an average Saturday morning so he had amused himself by being gallant to the first sap of a girl who had given him a chance.

It was time to stop this nonsense. Catrina straightened her bag, looped her scarf once and pushed her arms into the jacket that she had been sitting on for most of the day.

'You are leaving?'

Patrice had appeared at her side just as she became stuck, her arm caught in the sleeve half behind her back. She felt like a puppet chucked in the corner of the toy box.

'I should. I mean... thanks...'

'So soon.' It was a perfectly pleasant thing for Patrice to answer but Catrina immediately saw it as classic insincerity;

too smooth, too French.

'I have to.'

Patrice spread his hands in regret. 'That is sad. I finish here in ten minutes. I thought we could eat something.'

'Well...'

'Not here. I have had enough of the café today.'

'I ought to go home. There are things to do.'

'Yes, yes. Not a restaurant.'

'Perhaps...' Catrina had struggled into the jacket at last and was standing, though she realised the table was more helpful than it should have been.

'I could cook for you, for both of us.'

'Maybe I could call you? Later?'

Patrice looked crestfallen but began to look around for pen and paper. 'If that is what you want,' he said as he scribbled down a number and an email address on an old till receipt.

It was not at all what she wanted, Catrina realised as she picked up the paper and pushed into the depths of her shabby old bag. There was no way she would have the courage to call him. The rejection and hearing the pauses as he struggled to remember her voice would be too much to bear. She wondered if she would even have the nerve to use the Café Franck again;

the place where, until this afternoon, she had felt most calm and unbothered by emotional storms. Patrice was called back to take an order and she moved out from behind the table and down the two small steps to the bar level.

'Catrina. Wait. Please.'

She stopped. Patrice was wiping his hands and starting to take off his apron. From the other direction the curtains shielding the door from the wind shifted almost imperceptibly as the sliver that was Mariana sidled through. Catrina looked from one to the other. One she wanted to avoid and should talk to, the other she wanted never to avoid but couldn't talk to. She shook her head at Patrice, grinned weakly at Mariana and hurried out.

~~~

Oops

Louise Camille was enormous. It was not a matter of frites with everything, oceans of sauce over the top. She just was enormous and after an adolescence of diets, cycling, jogging, sweating and abstinence she had given up fighting it. Whatever her half French, half Martinesques, genes had in mind for her, they were not going to be deflected. Louise thought of herself as a moderate eater, eschewing cream cakes and tartes tatins with every meal, but admitted that she was a bit of a snacker and that slimline anything in gin tasted foul. There was just no escaping the fact that Louise tended to sail rather than walk.

Her passage was charted to navigate across the great expanses of the stone Place Flagey from the east side, while Saskia was just emerging from her haven of Ottoman empire food and rose water from the north west, a few dozen metres away.

From the Café Franck, at the corner of the old radio and TV building, Catrina was also emerging but in greater agitation than the Dutch woman on the far side. In fact their roles had been reversed as the day had worn on. Catrina's calm and good mood had disintegrated, Saskia had been lulled into fresh contentment after her ejection from the Franck and her adoption by the Levantine. Between them Louise glided serenely.

The two smaller women were having troubles with land transport. Saskia's path to the square was blocked by a pair of number 60 busses, making a rare weekend appearance and an even more rare simultaneous arrival in opposing directions. Catrina did not need to cross the road on her way home. She only needed to turn right along the side of the building but she wanted to clear her head after the crisis of a few moments before – the convergence of Mariana and Patrice at the bar demanding her attention. If she had been in less of a state she might have made for the shores of the large pond that graced the western flank of the square, as Louise intended to do, but she wanted anonymous space and air and she was not thinking where her feet were taking her until the urgent clanging of a tram's bell brought her up short at the kerb. She looked furiously at the pale yellow monster, daring it to crush her, then gave in to the inevitable and let it roll passed.

The tram's back end was almost clear when there was a shout from behind her. Catrina glanced back. Patrice was half out of the doorway, fixing the zip on his fleece jacket as he called.

Catrina panicked, she didn't know why. It was just, perhaps, that all the fun of the morning had left her with the beginnings of a hangover and the conviction that if she did not get away now, she would have to explain, make herself understood, look even more of a fool, feel wretched – all of it. She stepped across the tramlines and began to run.

'Catrina, wait,' Patrice yelled and darted after her. By the time he was over the road she was a third of the way across the square. So was Saskia, who looked up to see the two tormentors of the morning charging towards her. For a smug moment she imagined they had seen her leave the Café Levantine, realised their earlier behaviour was appalling and were sprinting to apologise. Well, apologise they might but 'sorry' was not a word that changed anything.

There was not a great deal of Catrina. Although her coat was too big and her bag was absurdly overstuffed, the actual frame of the English girl was slight. She thought of herself as a bundle of bones with random splatterings of flesh, as though they had been slapped on by a disinterested sculptor. She could generate speed though, even when tipsy and in the wrong shoes. Patrice cursed. You did not work long hours in the Café Franck without staying pretty lithe but even so, chasing girls literally was not something he had done much since he was thirteen.

Proceeding steadily with the calm assurance of a tanker oblivious to all but the severest swell, Louise was thinking that she preferred the square on Sundays, when it's open horizons were broken by the little market stalls and music booths, the scent of cheeses and the temptation of a vin chaud and freshly cooked titbits, waffles and brioches, little Turkish pastries and Algerian meatballs. As things stood, though, the sky was clouding over again and there was a nip to the teeth of the breeze, and half a ginger cake was waiting in her first floor apartment only a minute or two away on the other side of the pond. Louise looked down at her feet and pointed her prow into the wind.

The humiliation for Patrice was in the fact that Catrina felt she had to run from him, and that he was determined that she should not disappear before he had at least found out why. So he ran, and yelled as he ran. For a few seconds Catrina ignored him but then she realised what a spectacle she must be making as the line of citizens waiting at the tram and bus stops turned to watch – it was far more interesting than anything else on show.

She turned but she did not slacken pace. A second later there was a startled 'ooof' as shoulder bone met a yielding midriff. Catrina toppled forward, Louise toppled backwards and she just had the presence of mind to let her arm and knee take the brunt of the fall instead of her head. The crack as it met the stone impinged even on Catrina's shocked hearing.

'I'm so sorry,' she began inadequately as she rolled off the prone cushion that Louise had become, her eyes screwed shut in pain. Patrice arrived at the heap.

So, from the other direction, did Saskia. 'Pig,' she screamed at him, 'total pig.' Saskia stepped round the women on the ground and launched herself, hands shoving with all her outraged strength.

~~~

Above And Below

Fidel van der Looy was bored. The dalliance that he thought was possible with the delectable Elise from his evening in the theatre jazz bar and his morning at the Café Franck had come to nothing. Worse than that – it was, he realised, completely illusory. She had barely registered a flicker of recognition when he had made a carefully calculated foray to the counter for a lunchtime beer. He was, he knew too well at heart, just another old and misguided man stupid enough to mistake politeness for interest. His students hung on his every word, or pretended they did, and that was part of the problem.

Fidel loved attention, despite his shaggy hair, the deliberate stubble, the clothes from some 60s demo on the barricades of Paris (when he could fit into them – newer equivalents when he couldn't). That was the purpose of fame, however moderate, however professorial. That was why he did his best to haunt the minority programmes on tiny TV channels desperate for cheap punditry.

But it was Saturday afternoon. A film festival was due to start at seven and he had an invitation to the launch. Still three hours to kill, though.

What did people do on Saturdays, he wondered in all innocence? Wives, girls, daughters shopped, he supposed, and the first of those categories demanded that they be accompanied. Men watched football, of course. Fidel could talk about football – it was incumbent to his image as an intellectual with his instincts still rooted in the people – but the actual watching of a game truly horrified him. Now, a research project looking at the language yelled by those in the stands; that would have some interest, though the thought of having to get to a ground with the anonymous crowds, shout, sing and demonstrate support for one or other tribe distressed him.

There was reading, of course, or writing, though secretly Fidel's reputation as a great mind rested on the flimsy consumption of other people's words and a memory for good quotes. Books on sociology bored him as much, probably rather more, than the essays of those he taught. He would read if he had to but only because he needed to keep one chapter ahead of the class or because he wished to write a suitably excoriating review of a colleague's work and needed the ammunition.

He had read the newspapers and magazines for the day. He was not a man excited by novels. Television was something on which he like to appear but not to watch.

Writing was too hard. Fidel preferred talking.

For a minute or two the temptation was strong to get drunk, just a little, and wander up to the street alongside the Gare du Nord's tracks where the legal prostitutes sat on stools behind glass doorways. If he was spotted he could always say it was research for a new programme, an essay, an article. But it was an old excuse and one he had used before. Then he really had had to go and do the research and write the article. The reality of the girls' stories and the sheer loneliness of the other men had depressed him for weeks. Too close to the bone.

There was nothing for it, Fidel grumbled to himself as he crossed the tram tracks and headed up the hill on the northern side of the square. He would have to do the domestic chores that everybody assumed he had a mistress or a cleaning lady to do. It was Saturday. If he cleaned and dusted, laundered and hoovered, maybe the fates would send him someone at the film party to show it all to afterwards.

Once he had reconciled himself to the idea that he would be organising for the rest of the afternoon, Fidel's mood brightened. He paused in one of the Arab shops on the way home and bought himself some sweet cakes as a reward for when the flat was spruce and presentable.

The hill and the stairs were climbed, the door shoved open, the cakes dumped on the kitchen table and tea was brewed. With energy and surprising enthusiasm (which would have destroyed his public persona) he gathered brush, dust pan, hoover and turquoise feather duster and advanced into the sitting room. The energy evaporated as he looked around him. Clearly there was a stage or two to be gone through before actual cleaning was reached.

There were differences, he admitted as he began to shuffle papers and books from all across the floor, the low tables, the sofa and (most) around the circumference of his favourite armchair, between the adjectives intellectual, Bohemian and slovenly. In his case, sadly, all three applied.

Creating piles should create order.

As they proliferated, though, all the piles presented was a challenge to his categorising. And if his categorising remained challenged, what did that say about his ability to analyse, to enquire systematically, to conjure logic from the chaos of impressionistic opinion? In other words, if he couldn't tidy his sitting room without landing himself in a psychological maze with no exit then he was no sort of professor at all.

Fidel stood in the middle of the room, encircled by the new piles, his hands full and an article on Kant hanging from his teeth, and had an existential crisis.

The doorbell rang.

Of course it did. With a rising sense of panic Fidel looked at each of his handfuls in turn and squinted at the paper in his mouth, wondering which to put down, whether just to drop the lot and run to the door, or just ignore the wretched thing.

It was the drop that won. All the previous half hour of diligence was destroyed as the paper cascaded. Fidel reached the door and, looking more than slightly manic, flung it open. The mania turned to incredulity and his expression froze.

'Oh!' exclaimed the woman standing on the second floor landing, 'it's you.'

'Elise!' Fidel gathered himself. 'What a surprise.'

'Yes, I'm sorry.'

'Were you looking for me?'

'No, no. Not at all. I didn't even know you lived here.'

Fidel was disappointed but recovered his composure. 'Well, is there something...?'

'It's so strange. I've just moved in here,' Elise explained.

'Here?'

'Yes – below you. There is no name on your bell so I thought I would ring and find out who will be above me.'

Fidel did his best not to show the sheer explosion of fantasy the news unleashed. Instead he merely managed a smile.

'Come in.'

~~~

Slow Progress

The quartet grouped on the hard grey paving of Place Flagey could have been an interesting sculptural installation – or perhaps a piece of static performance art, since the objects were very clearly real people in various states of turmoil. Just for a moment, that instant of shock that always comes with collision and great emotion, the three women and one man were posed as a true tableau vivant. If Da Ponte and Mozart had been around they would have stopped the action right there for an ensemble in which the competing and conflicting thoughts of each character were given full vent: Louise's pained surprise, Catrina's embarrassment which seemed to be becoming a perpetual condition that tumultuous Saturday, Patrice's relief at catching Catrina before she fled, and Saskia's smug vindication now that Patrice and Catrina had proved themselves Barbarians.

As the moment of aria gave way to more prosaic recitative, Catrina and Patrice bent down to try to raise the immense form of Louise from the cold stone.

'I'm so sorry...' began Catrina fretfully and somehow with English inevitability. She was forestalled.

'Idiotic woman,' sneered Saskia. 'Can't you ever stop causing disasters? Wherever you are is the wrong place. Now just leave us alone and go away.' Her coldness was Arctic, quite enough to cause the tears to leap to Catrina's eyes.

That goaded Patrice into action once again. He hurdled

Louise and squared up to Saskia, so furious at her frigid Dutch self-righteousness that he wanted to break and flatten her stupid turned-up nose. His fist clenched, his arm drew back.

'Don't,' exploded Catrina, then as Patrice paused mid swing, pleaded, 'not about me, please.'

'Yes,' Saskia weighed in, 'I have had just about enough violence from you today.'

That was enough to get Catrina back on Patrice's side. 'Oh, jump in the lake, bitch,' she flared. 'That one over there will do fine.'

Meanwhile Louise was in too much pain either to follow the insults in English or to work out why there were people arguing over her. As Catrina took Patrice's arm and led him away, Louise looked up imploringly at Saskia. She needed help getting up and a kindly arm to lean on once she had. 'Si vous plais?' she asked.

Saskia had until that moment been enjoying her moral victory over her tormentors from the Café Franck too much to take any notice of the large female on the ground at her feet. Now though, she instinctively knew that any Good Samaritan gesture would nicely cement her feeling of vindication. Her dignity would be restored by the other's rise from the pavement. 'Of course,' she said, and proffered her hand.

There was uncertainty in Louise's eyes, though. Saskia looked sturdy enough but would she prove equal to the task? Louise's confidence was as shaky as her legs. In practice there was nothing to worry about. Saskia came from generations of sturdy Dutch farming stock and the muscles that in her grand-mother had shifted bales of hay without comment were well up to the task of hauling the young, if substantial, Walloon to her feet.

'Merci,' began Louise as she rose.

'Not a problem,' answered Saskia in English. Both in Belgium they might be but not even a good neighbourly gesture was these days going to bridge the language divide and induce the Dutch or the Fleming to lapse into French unless absolutely forced to do so. Her generation seemed to have picked up the same attitude to French that her Dutch sisters had adopted towards German after the Second World War – perfectly capable of understanding it but incapable of letting it pass her lips with good grace.

Louise, though, did not seem to mind. For one thing her knee and elbow hurt too much from being thumped to the ground. For another, she was not a language snob. If this blonde woman wanted to help her, which set of words she used in the process really didn't matter. She held on to the proffered arm as she tested the knee and winced.

'You are in pain,' announced Saskia, matter of factly.

'Yes but only for a moment I think,' said Louise optimisti-cally and took a step forward. 'Ow!'

'No – it will hurt for more than a moment, I'm afraid.' For the first time Saskia looked at Louise with a degree of sympathy unrelated to her being the victim of enemies. 'Where do you live?'

'Over there,' Louise let go of her knee to wave into the distance.

'Is it far, because if it is more than a few metres I think you should take a taxi.'

'No, no. Just the other side of the lake.' She took a step forward.

'Not without me, you can't,' said Saskia and began to lead her forward. It was slow going, even on the new paving of the square. Louise could feel the kneecap swelling even after a few paces and it really did not want to straighten or bear her weight.

On the street that bounded Place Flagey a trolley bus and a tram were just beginning to stop their progress from opposite directions but Saskia was having none of it. Imperiously she raised her hand and guided Louise into the path. There was a squeal of air brakes from the bus, a flurry of bells from the tram. Saskia strode, Louise hobbled, on.

The street commanded and conquered, they reached the side of the little lake and began to work their way around its muddy shore, Louise pointing the way to an apartment block about halfway along the long side of the water.

'I hope,' Saskia asked gently, 'you don't live at the top or, if you do, that there's a lift. I think we will be in trouble otherwise.' She was not just thinking of Louise's knee. She was thinking of her own condition if she tried to manoeuvre the considerable mass of the woman to the summit.

'No, I will be ok,' Louise assured her, smiling wanly as she read her thoughts, 'it is only one floor above the street. I can make it.'

'We both will.'

And they did.

~~~

Some Good Wine

'Sorry, it's a mess,' Catrina inevitably apologised as she shoved open the door to her miniscule flat. Had she been bigger, and had Patrice not been holding her by the waist and pushing gently forward, she might have barred the door until everything was tidy, clean and she could present her new lover (for that was what she now knew he was about to be) with the cool, sorted and together woman her ideal self image insisted was her natural state.

In truth, it was a mess, impressive by any standards. Patrice had the sense not to agree or let a flicker of amusement cross his features but this was a girl's room par excellence.

Instead, as Catrina fussed at trying to gather the strewn clothes into heaps of at least generic order (tops and jumpers, skirts and trousers, shoes, knickers and socks – there only seemed to be one spare bra, she realised absently), he tactfully made for what passed as a kitchen, shoved aside the unwashed detritus and started to find the makings of coffee.

In the corner by some stale bread (and a pot of something called 'Marmite', which he sniffed and rejected with a shudder) he spotted a bottle of red wine. He examined it as the water heated. Costières de Nîmes, 2008. Could be all right – in fact could be quite good if it was not too thin. Did Catrina know about wine, he wondered, or was it a happy accident? If she did know what to look for without spending a fortune then it was not only a pleasant surprise, he would have to revise his stereotypical view of the English.

He peered back into the main room. 'Coffee, or you have some good wine? Or perhaps coffee and wine?'

It was yet another urgent but unnecessary decision and Catrina was not good at those, he was coming to realise. She was standing at the end of the bed holding the bottoms of a pair of flowery pyjamas and caught between shame at their domestic unfashionability and trying to give an opinion that she didn't have. She looked up at Patrice and her hands dropped to her sides.

He read her. 'It does not matter. Not now,' he said and ignored the boiling kettle.

'Sure?'

'Who needs to choose?' Patrice came close, touched her

cheek with the back of his fingers for a second, then kissed her. Catrina gave no resistance but her hands hung limply, still holding the frayed pyjamas.

She stayed exactly the same as Patrice kissed harder, as he slipped off her jacket and let it fall, reached up the back of her baggy T-shirt to unclip her bra, and found and dealt with the button on her jeans. There was no resistance but no comment either as he swapped their positions, unzipped himself, and fell backwards onto the bed, tipping her on top of him. She marvelled how in seconds, despite still being dressed – in the sense that nothing was completely off – they were locked together.

It was not that she didn't want to make love, or didn't know what to do, or didn't care enough to enjoy it. Catrina was just revelling in letting things take their course without needing any initiative from her. Patrice seemed to understand, or if he didn't, was enjoying himself too much to care. He guided, cajoled, and arranged her with exquisite timing and gentleness.

This, Catrina thought at a moment in their love making that should have been devoid of thought, was not Bruno the computer nerd all hump, smug and doctrine, or her fraught and lovelorn university washouts, or the ghastly grope from the old bloke at the Parliament; this was late Saturday afternoon in heaven.

They never did find a taste for coffee that night but the wine was eventually opened and Patrice approved. It was warm and fruity, as befitted a southern bottle, and complemented their second, more conventional bout of caresses. As it was sipped away so their energy dipped and they drifted, napping in each other's arms until either hunger or the slamming of doors on other floors woke them in the dark. It was not after eight, they found.

They lay, content with this new reality, unimagined only ten hours before, and snuggled under the duvet. An autumn shower scattered against the window and Catrina burrowed deeper against Patrice. She was hungry, now, so hungry. But the thought of disturbing this nest of man and bedding was beyond her. Perhaps she could linger like this forever, her body metamorphosed into a state above human, needing nothing except what she had now. She sighed, then giggled at the thought of herself as a Greek nymph.

That tore it. Patrice shifted. 'You are laughing at me!' he announced, just a little shocked.

'No, no - at me, at how happy I am,' Catrina placated, not wholly successfully. It was surely too complicated to explain the vision of her garlanded, her hair in a silk band, a diaphanous transparent dress billowing in a breeze rising from the Peloponnese.

She hugged him hard but after a few minutes of rather automatic stroking Patrice disengaged himself and found his way to the cupboard that served as her bathroom. She heard bottles and oddments being moved and then the experimental running of the shower. If he could work out how to get and keep it hot without scalding or freezing himself alternately, then he was quite a guy.

Evidently he did because, after five minutes, he emerged fresh and with no obvious burn marks and perched naked on the side of the bed.

Catrina studied him for the first time and decided she couldn't believe her luck. But she just said, 'Maybe we should eat, what do you think?'

'Here?' Patrice did not sound convinced, forgetting that a few hours earlier, in their old pre-lover lives, he had suggested coming to the flat instead of a restaurant.

'Nothing here to eat except old bread.'

She was not sure if she was pleased with the hint of relief in her new lover's voice as he said, 'then we will go out. We have much to celebrate.'

~~~

Vespers

As Saturday drew to a close the Café Franck had a totally different crowd in. Fidel and Elise gave it hardly a glance as they ambled out of the cinema in the old broadcasting studios of the main building and made their way home. Elise had taken his arm, which pleased Fidel more than anything that had happened to him in months, possibly even that year.

Perhaps more than his purring at the glory of coincidence

that had seen their encounter move in twenty-four hours from theatre bar, to café service, to doorway surprise, to film festival launch and now to the wander home, Fidel's joy was unleashed when he found that Elise's chosen university field of Circus Studies had not prevented her from taking on the cynical coterie of French intellectuals who gravitated to Fidel at any party. More than taken them on, in fact had utterly trounced them. Fidel had said little himself, partly in case he let himself in for a trouncing, and had just smiled enigmatically and left the mind field to her. Elise was tiny in body but big in brain and not afraid to use it in attack. The floor of the Flagey foyer was littered with the wine cups of her conquests.

The only question that remained was whether she would say goodnight in front of her door, at his one floor up from hers, or forget the goodnight altogether and let Fidel guide her into bed.

Across the lake from Flagey arts centre Louise Camille was still aching. The first ache was in her knee, on which she had fallen so thunderously that afternoon. The second ache was in her back, on which she had been lying for much of the time since, and the third ache was in her conscience, much troubled by how and whether it was wise that she – profoundly hetero-sexual in all her French fantasies up to now – had found herself making love to a very fit Dutch girl who communicated only in English when she bothered to speak at all.

Saskia, the fit one in question, was equally bemused by what she had done. The wine they had shared – anaesthetic for Louise in theory – had eased the path but she was still amazed that, in the act of helping the large woman to undress so that she could bandage the injured knee, rather more had come off than either of them had been expecting.

Now she lay by her new lover, gazed at the damp patch high above in the corner of the white ceiling, and wondered where it was all going to lead. More urgently she wondered whether to get dressed and head for home or stay and see what the cool light of Sunday morning brought along.

Among the Spaniards there was discord. They had found a very uninspiring tapas bar by accident after getting onto the wrong tram and heading in the opposite direction from the park under the Atomium at Heysel. Eventually the male three of the quartet had made their way there, after the early after-noon rain had passed, but by then Mercedes was tired of all her companions, Jose, Jordi and Joaquin. She had left them to their own devices after lunch, taken the right tram back to her flat near to Midi station, bathed the scalded shoulder in tepid water and gone to sleep.

She had woken, hungry, at eight and called all three on their mobiles but none had answered. By the time she finally reached them at ten it was clear they were between bars and well beyond eating anything civilised. She raided the fridge for salami, found some bread, olives and fruit tea and settled down in her dressing gown to sulk.

For her men, there was nothing but contention. What else could it be after a day of drinking beer far stronger than anything at home in Spain?

The relative merits of the managers of the Valencia and Atletico Madrid football teams soon widened to cover everything that support implied: the quality of the squads, the politics that the clubs represented, whether it was better to live in the capital or by the sea, the impossibility of one finding a single attractive woman in the vicinity of the other, and the minimal standards of manhood that was clearly the problem if you could. If they had been loud in the morning, by the time they were ushered out of Au Mort Subite they were yelling. But the difference, perhaps, between them and the more northern inebriates spilling onto the pavement some time after midnight was that, once on the pavement, the shouting stopped, arms gripped each other's shoulders and the only debate was how on earth to find their way back to Mercedes' flat.

Mariana, now a parliamentary assistant but in her estimation of her future one of Finland's true global activists, had spent the evening discussing the necessity of veganism in a world dominated by climate change and that only a society from which manure and its gasses was eliminated could save us.

Actually Mariana hadn't discussed anything herself. That had been taken care of by the three older women and one

ravenous male sage on the platform in the European Association of Pulse Growers who were hosting a Bean and Pea Weekend. Mariana had tried to be converted, she tried really hard,
but in the end the awfulness of the lentil and goji berry juice
cocktail that was all that was on offer at the end had sent her
mournfully home to a surreptitious bottle of rosé and a long
online moan to the man in South Carolina she was beginning
to think of as the only friend who properly understood her.

On the other hand her boss, Esko Nystrom MEP was, much
to his surprise, finishing his Saturday evening in a jazz bar next
to Flagey where the light was bad and the music raucous, on
his umpteenth glass of bad vin de table, crushed against a
French film starlet.

It had started at the film festival opening, to which
naturally he found he had an invitation lurking in his briefcase,
since he was a substitute on the Parliament's Culture Committee. Had they felt bold enough, Fidel and Elise would have
liked to have told him that his head had prevented them seeing
much of the brunette starlet in question's finest performance
in the screening that had followed the reception.

As it was Esko had understood barely a word of the film
and had little opinion of the female lead other than that she
mumbled, though the rest of her seemed attractive enough.

At the second reception of the evening, this time much smaller and in a secluded side room, he had taken no notice whatever of the small blonde girl entering ahead of him. He had also been too busy deciding between doubtful champagne and red wine that was not much better to see who the clapping was for. He vaguely assumed the director must be there some-where and looked around for a tray of canapés.

The festival's organiser had scurried across, grabbed the star by both hands and, after voluble congratulations, looked round for somebody suitably important to introduce her to. His eyes fell on Esko.

'Mr. Nystrom, so glad you could be with us this evening. Meet Amelie,' he had announced and spun away to greet more examples of greatness.

'Hello.'

'Hello.' He looked down.

'Nystrom,' savoured Amelie, 'are you from Sweden?'

'Finland. And you?'

Amelie looked a touch surprised but just said, 'French of course. And what do you do in Finland?'

'Not very much these days,' admitted Esko, 'I'm a Member of the European Parliament here. What do you do?'

This time Amelie was truly baffled. 'Um, I'm an actress.'

Esko looked suitably concerned. 'Hard to get work these days, I suppose.'

'I'm lucky.'

'Will I have seen you in anything? I'm afraid I don't watch

much television here.'

Amelie was trying to decide if he was being deliberately rude but thought she ought to give it one more try. 'You just have.'

Esko's brow furrowed. 'Have I? I'm sorry, what was your name again?'

'Amelie,' she paused. 'Amelie Poitiers.'

The Parliamentarian blinked, closed his eyes for a second, imagining that there would be no-one in sight when he opened them. The actress was still there, still real. 'Oh hell. But your hair....'

'Dyed two weeks ago. Another film.'

'I'm so sorry, I just wasn't expecting, concentrating...' his apology petered out.

'No. It's great.' She was smiling mischievously. 'You really didn't recognise me?' Esko shook his head. 'I'm so pleased. It means I have a chance of getting around without getting followed everywhere.'

'Still, I really should...'

Amelie broke in. 'Do you think you could take me out of here?'

'Certainly.'

'For a drink, somewhere without many lights? Near?'

Esko looked at his half tasted bad Bordeaux. 'Without doubt.'

Which is why an hour later Amelie was on a high stool and Esko was standing jammed against her thigh fifty metres away from the doors of Flagey as they drank too much and fought about politics.

III

Monday

The Realities Of Monday

The Mickey Mouse Coffee Bar of the European Parliament had been aptly named by one of the first Green members, a German utterly unimpressed by the gravity of his office, who likened the multicoloured chair backs to that rodent's ears. Sadly both the chair backs (with some colour variations that even the most extreme of Europe's potty parties had never adopted) and the German Green had both been ejected in favour of something less stylish. Among the assistants at least the epithet had remained, however, and one set of the chairs was roped off at the entrance to recall the story.

It was, for most of the week, the preferred hang-out for MEPs and lobbyists of all shades because it was on the same floor and right next to the main debating chamber. But at nine o'clock on a Monday morning there were no MEPs. They would still all be in their own countries or on the way back from weekend speaking missions and nobody expected to see them till afternoon. And if there were no MEPs there were no lobbyists either.

Mickey Mouse was doing brisk business, though. The queue for the café normal and croissants was two deep in assistants, stagiares and administrators. Saskia had elbowed her way to the front, demanded a large coffee with extra milk in loud Dutch, and stomped to a window seat.

It had been a ridiculous and probably disatrous weekend. Her romantic explorations with Louise had carried her through half of Sunday until her greatest desire had proved to be a shower in her own flat and fresh clothes. The parting had felt embarrassing to Louise and sentimental (which was worse) to Saskia.

A night in her own bed had failed to restore her good temper and now she was faced with a day of fixing the catering and printing for three fruitless meetings organised by the political grouping she worked for, the United European Regional Nationalists (UERN), known by its opponents as the Urinals.

A little behind Saskia the equally disenchanted Mariana waited her turn and ordered a café au lait and, far too early by French standards, a salmon baguette. If she couldn't smoke, which she couldn't without going out of the building into the damp park and fighting her way back through security again, then she wanted to eat. She paid and grunted with the bass notes that only a Finnish woman of her age commands naturally before shoving her way back through the throng and to a window seat at the further end of the windows from Saskia.

A few seconds later Catrina strolled in and looked at the crowd with consternation. She was in the best mood that was possible that early on a Monday. Walking was a trifle harder trial than usual, though, for Patrice had taught her rather more than a better French accent almost continuously, her inner thighs told her, since Saturday evening. But her happiness levels were higher than she could remember – well, at least since her second year at university. The world, Catrina felt, should allow her instant and unfettered access to breakfast since there had been nothing left in her kitchen and Patrice had left at six to go to his own place, change, and be back serving at the Café Franck at Flagey by eight.

The world, however, had different ideas, and remained a solid multicultural barrier between Catrina and the counter. She dithered, grimaced, and eventually dived for a miniscule gap between a pair of Italians and something male that might have been Bulgarian.

She emerged armed with a capuccino that she could have swum in, together with both a croissant and a pain au chocolat and headed out into the main body of the bar in front of the windows.

A glance told her that all but one of the seats were taken. She was in no mood to hang around waiting for some man to gazump her and strode for it as fast as the balancing of her coffee would allow. She was so intent on not spilling it that she only looked up at who might be across the table once she had sat down and gingerly placed the cup and saucer on the table.

'Oh god,' she gasped.

From the other side of the table Saskia looked at the new arrival with a mixture of astonishment and instinctive loathing. She said nothing, however, and gazed at the leaves falling from the trees in the Parc Leopold beneath her.

'I'm sorry,' began Catrina instinctively. 'I just saw it was empty. I didn't notice you were here.'

Saskia lazily turned back to Catrina with icy eyes. 'That seems to be the way we usually meet.'

'I suppose you work here too.'

'Yes,' Saskia had no desire to elaborate. It was bad enough having this ridiculous Englishwoman in the same building.

Catrina, though, felt the social niceties had to be observed or there would be a feud, and after all, if it hadn't been for the woman opposite, she would never have ended up in the arms of Patrice. 'I'm Catrina, by the way.'

'Really.'

'And you?'

'Saskia van Leuven.'

'Saturday was a bit of a mess, I'm afraid. At least the part of it when we met.' Catrina felt it was enough of an apology to break the ice.

Saskia's literal mind, used to Dutch uncompromising directness, just thought it was futile inability to confront what had taken place, either in Café Franck or on the paving outside. So she just shrugged and finished her coffee.

Catrina ploughed on, her mouth full of pastry and chocolate. 'I hope the rest of your weekend was better?'

The Dutchwoman rose to her feet and the wave of stiffness in protesting muscles hit her. She winced. 'Possibly,' she managed to say between gritted teeth. She had no intention of letting Catrina probe any further, gathered her handbag and strode off without another word.

Normally such a curt brush-off would have filled Catrina with buckets of self doubt and remorse but Patrice had banished all that, at least for the next few hours. In turn, she banished thoughts of Saskia and turned to the prospects for the morning. The dreaded Belstead, her Europhobic Tory boss, would be arriving at around midday, she reckoned. He always pretended he was rushing back on the early train after a hard weekend in his regional office. Catrina knew that he usually made it as far as Paris, where he alternated between his mistress's apartment in Montparnasse and a spot of cottageing with some rough stuff in the Marais.

The thought of him was enough to make her need more coffee: very black this time, sans lait and with extra sugar.

~~~

Opening Shots

Esko Nystrom, MEP from Finland, had never taken his duties as a substitute member of the Committee for Education, Youth, Culture and Sport (described sneeringly by those on Budget and Foreign Relations as the 'Any Other Business' Committee) very seriously. His main sphere of interest and seat of influence was the Justice and Citizenship Committee, closely followed by Health and Environment. He was changing the world on those, at least a little, he felt: but on the Culture Committee? Surely that was just about keeping the world entertained and possibly musicians moving.

Since early on Sunday morning, however, he had discovered a new enthusiasm for its relevance. Encountering Amelie Poitiers in a starring role on screen had done little for him. Spending much of the rest of the night in her company (though sadly not quite enough to be newsworthy, he thought) had convinced him that his support for European film was utterly essential.

The Culture Committee was due to meet on Tuesday and by 10am that Monday morning Esko had phoned his surprised colleague in Finland and persuaded him not to turn up so that Esko could. Scanning the agenda, he was pleased to see that it was the final budget meeting that would decide how much help would be given in the coming year.

He looked at the papers and frowned over his muesli. The negotiated line of his party was to vote against. No chance. Too late to table an amendment adding a few million but he was certainly going to vote for the highest amount on offer, the French Green Party's double the current line. It might infuriate his own party hacks but it would be his first line of defence when he met Amelie for dinner the following evening, whatever the outcome of the vote.

The diary was not full. Everybody, including his assistant Mariana, expected him to be out of the office that morning. He should be on a flight from either Finland or Moldova. In theory he could loaf around, amble into the Café Franck for coffee and newspapers, find a non-parliamentary date for lunch, and head for the first scheduled meeting at four. It was tempting but Esko was a Finn with a sense of duty and besides, he couldn't think of anybody he wanted to see except Amelie and she was back in Paris, he assumed.

Whistling virtuously, he climbed the hill up to Avenue Louise and hopped on the 54 bus to Place Luxembourg.

Mariana was staggered to see him appear in the office, high in G tower, shortly before eleven carrying a large carry-out coffee. She peered at him suspiciously as he grinned and passed on through to the inner office without a word.

There was nothing unusual about the silence but the grin and the coffee was. She left him alone for a few minutes while she composed her thoughts and went through the diary and urgent papers to see if there was something she had missed. He hadn't gone away for the weekend, that she knew from their encounter in the Café on Saturday, but the sight of him on a Monday morning was as much a disturbance to her routine as to his.

After a decent interval, in which she half expected him to emerge and explain himself, Mariana pushed back her chair and went to lean against the door frame.

'Everything OK?' she asked.

Esko looked up from his computer where he was sorting through the email inbox.

'Yes, fine. Why?'

'Well, it's....'

'It's what?'

'Monday.'

'I know.' Esko went back to scrolling down the emails. For a few seconds Mariana held her position, expecting something more by way of explanation. It didn't come. Her shoulders slumped in resignation and she did her best to scowl as she strode back to her own desk. She was even more indignant when Esko came to shut the connecting door a few minutes later.

She picked up the phone extension when she heard him talking. Nothing. He must be using his mobile. The scowl became a full scale frown. Mariana hated being left out.

On her screen were the voting positions agreed by the group leaders on all the committee motions and amendments tabled for the following three days. Concentrating was hard but then Mariana thought of a subtle little act of revenge. She made a new copy of the amendments file and changed the instruction on every third one – a no to yes, more usually a yes to a no. Then she printed out just one copy and deleted the file. Esko would be the only one with that paper and she wouldn't give it to him. It would be left on her desk when she left for the evening. If he picked it up and used it, there'd be hell to pay. If not, there'd be no harm done. It had been just a draft that she had never given to him and had meant to shred. A nice calculation.

The phone rang. She waited for the light to come on her set to show that Esko had picked up but it didn't. He was probably still on his mobile call. She let it ring six times then deigned to lift the receiver.

'Esko Nystrom's office,' she answered in English. The reply was brisk and in Finnish. 'Oh, Rikka – yes he's at his desk. Hold on, I'll get him.' Mariana didn't bother to patch the call through. She pushed opened the door and said loudly in English, 'Your wife's on the phone.'

The startled look on Esko's face was satisfaction enough. Mariana sat down again behind her desk, leaving the door open so that she could hear the hurried goodbye, which turned out not to be quite as hurried or as guilt ridden as she had been hoping – and in English. She watched as Esko put away his mobile and picked up the office phone before replacing her own handset. Then Esko moved towards her and gently but firmly shut the door again.

Had she gone too far? Was she feeling hurt and vindictive because she had been ignored on Saturday and had a miserable weekend trying to be interested in the politics of Veganism? Or was she just put out by having her uncluttered Monday morning turned into just another day with the boss in the office? And if she had gone too far, how and was this war?

~~~

Elise Considers

Elise looked at herself naked in the long bedroom mirror and was unconvinced. There was nothing to her to be convinced about really: legs too thin, scrawny arse, chest that barely made it to being female, straggly brown hair. Hard to imagine what her new lover, as Fidel seemed to be, could get obsessive about. She tugged viciously at a stray tuft of hair and began to dress. Nothing was unpacked yet – well, stuff was unpacked in the sense that it was in piles strewn across the floor. She consoled herself with the thought that she had been installed for less than three days while Fidel's apartment upstairs was in not much better shape. The only real difference was that his floor was covered with papers not clothes. She would have to do something about his clothes, she decided as she rummaged for a clean bra. He might be a famous intellectual and an icon of free thinking but there were remnants of t-shirts that would disgrace a tramp.

Fidel! What on earth had got into her? He was not the first

middle-aged man to chat her up when she was working behind the bar. There was one virtually every night. Nor was he the first to follow her with his eyes as she emerged from the Café Franck's kitchen to gather dishes or wipe tables. Even with her unsensational figure she was used to men scrutinising her as she bent to the task. On the other hand he was the first to invite her to a film festival premiere and, much, much more importantly, the first man with a reputation to take her ideas seriously and introduce her to his impressive friends as an equal. Now that was really new.

Even so, perhaps she would not have stayed the night that first time in normal circumstances. But there was nothing normal about this. He lived upstairs, he had just let her follow him if she wanted, and then they had carried on with better champagne than the festival party could offer.

Elise picked a rather flirtatious top. She intended to express her new status as the girlfriend of a great man actively – a little bright colour here, a touch of lace there, maybe that skirt that was just a centimetre or five too short.

From upstairs came the sound of footsteps pacing back and forth. Fidel was thinking too. After a few minutes, and a couple of hundred clunks across the ceiling, Elise looked up and frowned as she searched for the right shoes.

That was the key. If Fidel was going to think, and if he needed to walk to think, he would have to do so without shoes. Otherwise the rhythm of those steps would drive her mad or alternatively they would have to swap apartments and that was not going to happen. Perhaps there was a compromise. He could sleep in hers and only be allowed upstairs to think once she had left for college or the café.

Monday was a college morning, nothing too searching, thank heavens. Her lecturers had come to a reasoned understanding with the students that Modern Circus Studies would not include practical work on a Monday morning. Too many fingers had been burned (not to mention wigs, tassels and tutus) through lack of co-ordination after the weekend before. The substitute was not much of an improvement, Elise decided as she mounted her bicycle and headed off on the winding journey to her faculty. The subject of the morning's discourse was to be 'trapeze as a metaphor for emotional risk'. She rather suspected Fidel would have wiggled the high wire until they all fell off.

Fidel himself was soon on the tram aiming for the Sociology Department, not to teach but to add his gravity to an internal meeting on whether it was ethical to accept suggestions for research topics from government – particularly when the minister of education in question from the Flemish community was known to have nationalist views that would have made even his venomous party seem mild in the wilder reaches of the Balkans. The view should be, Fidel had every intention of expounding, that doing the research was fine as long as the results proved the bastard conclusively wrong on every point. Knowing his colleagues and the vagaries of the discipline as he did, there was not much chance of getting the money anyway.

Before going into the meeting in the faculty Fidel ambled up a floor and shoved open the door of his office, the office he had occupied now for nineteen years and which was a monument of stale cigarette smoke and curling theses to the hours of study and snoozing that gone into the acquisition of his present status.

Fidel raised his eyes from the door handle and froze in shock.

Clean!

Not just clean. Painted! And painted sky blue in that thoroughly bilious colour beloved of new parents expecting a boy for the first time. Cleared shelves, the desk on its head, scuffed legs in the air like a dead spider. Che Guevara's poster was rolled and sticking out of one of the thirty boxes into which every book and paper, every ashtray and paperclip had been efficiently dumped.

The professor bellowed. It was the sound of an enraged intellect or, as his grinning colleague Wilfred Tinnemans decided two doors down, the sound an ox makes when the cowman slips a tight rubber ring round its balls. The meeting was going to be a lot of fun. Tinnemans weighed up the chances of the Head of Department getting beyond point two on the agenda and was prepared to bet a bottle of Duval to the virginity of ten undergraduates that he'd be lucky to speak five words in the allotted two hours.

Three streets away Elise ventured the opinion that trapeze was not only a cathartic resolution of emotional risk, it was an essential component of the release from everyday frustration and the aspiration of the human spirit. Drivel of course, but she'd had two nights with Fidel to learn how to score points off those with limited brain power and no sense of humour.

~~~

Unparliamentary Business

On Monday Esko Nystrom's world was just splendid, despite the unsettling call from Rikka, his wife. To have a quiet day in the office unmolested by lobbyists, colleagues in the European Parliament or other Finns was a rare joy. He had grunted at Mariana, encouraged her to go for as long a lunch as possible, and settled down to read all those reports that a politician promises he has digested thoroughly but of which he hardly ever gets beyond the synopsis and the recommendations. By four o'clock he had mulled and mused, notated and commented, emailed and texted so that party co-ordinators and committee secretaries had wondered whether he was obsessed or, more likely, intending to run for one of the plum party jobs that would come up before Christmas. If this was the volume of work he was going to generate, they profoundly hoped not.

In between there was still time for a little daydreaming, though, and even a quick trawl of the internet for download-able snippets and the back catalogue of Amelie Poitiers, the lovely French actress he had encountered, drunk with till the early hours, but failed to bed on Saturday night. As he perused a particularly revealing clip from a scene filmed four years earlier, he could wait no longer.

He reached for his mobile and dialled the newly treasured number.

The voice was all there, the velvet French, the elisions of a girl in a hurry, the attempt to sound businesslike, but the person was not. Esko felt his smile freeze and his heart sink as he was directed to voicemail. He summoned up his best French – never entirely convincing – hoped her day was going well and that she was still prepared to meet him on Tuesday evening.

A few minutes later the heart was back on song as the texted reply came through. She was so sorry she hadn't picked up the phone. She hadn't recognised the number. Could he call again?

Esko pressed the button.

'Esko?' she answered. The velvet voice seemed to have matured into liquid praline.

'Bien sûr.'

'Let's stick to English, darling, then we won't make little mistakes.'

'Of course,' he said again. In reality there was nothing else he wanted to say. Listening and agreeing was quite enough for now.

'Listen,' Amelie began, unnecessarily for once, 'I can't do tomorrow now. My agent has booked me in for some stupid chat show. I hate them but the film people insist.'

Esko's whole day collapsed. 'Oh. What a shame. Still, I understand.' He nearly added 'of course' but actually there was no longer any of course about it. Understanding was proving a bit of a struggle.

'But it doesn't matter, does it? I mean...'

Yes it does, Esko thought. It matters a hell of a lot. The prospect of seeing her again had knocked twenty years, make it thirty, off his age. He felt, or had felt until this last bomb-shell, just as he had when he was a teenager and the best looking girl in his class had agreed to sit next to him on the bus after school.

'Of course not,' he answered, 'I'm sure there will be other...'

Amelie sounded as crestfallen as him now. 'Oh, I see. You must be terribly busy. I was hoping you could make it tonight instead. But...'

'Tonight!' Esko shouted, disconcerting his film starlet even further. 'Of course. Tonight. Yes, yes, yes.'

'OK,' she sounded a little wary at the vehemence. 'What time will you be free?'

Esko looked at the door of his office for a second and eased out from behind the desk. 'Wait. I'll check.' He laid the phone down and opened the door. Mariana was squinting at the email inbox as usual.

'Could you do me a favour? Could you go down to Ritva's office and see if she's got the notes she wanted me to see on the ACP film industry resolution?'

Mariana frowned. 'Now, I mean, can't I wait for the email?'

'Now please, they're handwritten and I want to take them home in a minute.'

His assistant shrugged and strode off, the irritation some-how expressed by her spikey hips as she walked.

Esko grinned and went back to his desk, locking the door behind him.

'That would be wonderful. I'm clear as soon as you want,' he said back into his mobile.

'Good boy,' purred his actress. 'Give me an hour.'

'Where are you?'

'The Conrad but I really don't want you here. The lobby is always crawling with paparazzi.'

'There's no point coming here, either,' agreed Esko. What about my flat - just across the road from Flagey. We could have a drink then go up to Lucio's on Avenue Louise for dinner.'

'Parfait.'

Esko gave her the address. 'But make it two hours. I should

finish up here and shower. Tidy a bit too.'

'That goes for me as well. Fine. 6.30.' Amelie rang off.

Mariana's day became even more baffling when she made it back from the other MEP's office, clutching a handful of scrawled notes. The easy-going, studious calm of the afternoon had been replaced by a tornado. Esko shoved the papers into his briefcase, clasped her round the shoulders in thanks, and bolted from his office as if late, very late, for a crucial vote.

A few hours later, but earlier than the excellence of Lucio's chef regarded as due reverence for his art, the Finnish MEP and the French actress lay together and stared at the high ceiling, his hand gently stroking the translucent down on her arm. Now nothing at all, at least nothing outside the two square metres of Esko's bed mattered very much.

Elsewhere in Brussels professionals were busy. There were deals to be done, negotiations to be finished in minutes, subsidiary rights to be agreed, stories to sell and careers to make or break. New lovers might step off the world for an evening but they could in the process make that of others spin faster.

~~~

Brain Power

Patrice's Monday shift behind the bar of the Café Franck finished at six and in truth it had dragged. There was never much of a crowd on a Monday – the unemployed regulars, of course, the lunchtime flurry of young mothers, the occasional drop-ins for a business meeting of those who didn't have or were escaping from an office. Even they had all seemed thinner on the ground than usual. The shift had really dragged because Patrice was not concentrating on it; his brain power was devoted to higher things, or perhaps lower things, depending on which aspect of Catrina he was considering at the time.

In the final quarter of an hour, however, a series of arrivals distracted him and pulled him back to café life.

First to drift in was the silver maned figure of Hugo de Greef, a big beast of the Belgian arts scene who had once been the boss of all the halls and studios that made up the Flagey complex. Hugo eased to the bar, demanded a mint tea (in itself a shock to Patrice who had half filled a glass with a favourite beer already) and progressed to a distant corner. He was followed there a few minutes later by the long stride of Kathrin Deventer and her staff from the European House of Culture: an Italian, a Portuguese and someone who could have been Polish.

All ordered the same as Hugo. The box of fresh, or at least defrosted, mint was disappearing fast. Patrice expected rather better of the Portuguese and the Italian at least. They, on the other hand, had long given up on the miniscule tumblers of acid vin plonk that Café Franck thought good enough for customers who resisted Belgian beer.

Patrice was immune to most of the tasks he had to undertake behind the bar but he had a particular aversion to making the mint tea – unless, he was newly prepared to admit, it was for Catrina. Without her ordering it they might never have got so close. But still, the task was a trial of any barman's patience.

Instead of dunking a sprig or two and a tea bag into a cup like most establishments did, the manager of the Café Franck had decreed that it should be a full performance. A thick beer glass had to be wrapped in a paper napkin folded into a triangle, which was secured with a twist of the angles at its hypotenuse. Mint was then extracted from a plastic bin, a long-handled tea pod had to be filled from a tin on a high shelf, and hot water poured. Then two sachets of sugar were to be threaded through the coil of the pod's handle and a single biscuit tucked into the napkin. By the time he had done this four times in a row the queue of real drinkers waiting to be served had grown lengthy and impatient.

For every mint tea he served, Patrice knew that he was about to confront three grumpy partakers of alcohol.

Five minutes to go, then he could slip out and wait for Catrina with his own first drink of the day.

The second surprise was to see Fidel enter and, his face like thunder, order a large cognac instead of taking a small 'blanche' to his regular solitary space. With the most cursory of nods, he hurried across to Hugo's table of cultural administrators – a breed (he could not bring himself to call it a profession) he usually loathed. When Patrice's colleague Elise, whom he had not seen since Saturday and knew was not due to work in the café until the following evening, came in, smiled at him without ordering, and went to throw her arm round Fidel's neck as he talked to Hugo, he was truly baffled.

One minute to go.

He spotted Catrina getting off a bus across the square. What sixth sense had made him glance outside at just that moment, he wondered? Often he could go the whole shift without noticing the world outside, even the weather.

Catrina's face opened in happiness as she arrived at the bar.

'Your timing is perfect,' Patrice greeted her. 'At this instant we can both have a drink – as long as it is not mint tea.'

Before Catrina could answer him, though, Kathrin's hand reached down and tapped her shoulder.

'Hi.'

Catrina looked round, then up. 'Oh – hi,' she said in friendly recognition, then in a fluster of English propriety, pointed across the bar. 'This is Patrice, Patrice this is Kathrin. She...'

'We know,' they both answered.

'I'm just over there,' Kathrin gestured. 'Come and join us.'

'Oh, well...' Catrina glanced uncertainly at Patrice.

He waved her off. 'Go ahead. I will join you in a minute. I

have to finish and log out anyway.'

When they had all gathered and explained the interconnec-
tions, Patrice reflected that so much had changed in a few days
that the café's scene was barely recognisable from a week before. Back then, it transpired, Kathrin had known Catrina from
lobbying the Parliament and Hugo had known Fidel because
big intellectual beasts always knew each other in a country the
size of Belgium. But since then Fidel had met Elise, Patrice had
fallen for Catrina and so the circle was complete.

Only Fidel looked glum. Hugo and Kathrin were radiating
understanding, Elise was holding his hand protectively as he
told them of the agony of finding his office invaded, tidied,
painted, even (and he almost spat as he uttered the words used
by the head of department) cleaned and improved.

Fidel subsided and gradually calmed under the influence
of Elise's reassuring fingers.

'Maybe you should change university?' suggested Hugo.

'You mean resign?' Fidel was incredulous. 'Where would I
go, after all these years?'

'Anywhere would be proud to have you,' soothed Elise and
Catrina nodded.

Kathrin looked across at both the eminences grises. 'Maybe
you should both start a new one?'

They stared back and guffawed.

'I'm serious.'

It was Patrice who said the fateful words.

'Why not?'

~~~

Resolution

On Monday evening Louise Camille tidied up her desk later than usual. Her contract as a Social Assistant, in the Brussels Welfare Office that loomed over Place Flagey almost as loftily as the great arts complex itself, stated that she could leave at four-thirty, assuming of course that she had arrived promptly at eight-thirty in the morning. But that day she had not, she had been hobbling a little, tidying the flat as best she could, and nursing the other parts of her body that had enjoyed such unexpected excitement, thanks to Saskia, over the weekend. Her knee still hurt like hell and her elbow was bruised to a vivid purple.

The result of lateness was a desk load of case work, all of which needed reading, annotating and stamping before it was handed over for more action or, the likelier outcome, instant filing for oblivion.

In reality doing the work in the hour and a half after everybody else had left the office was a delight and meant that she got through it in half the normal time and with twice the normal satisfaction. Louise was a conscientious woman who genuinely believed in the help she was able to give those left on the scrap heap of society. She might not be able to do much, and she knew that the Belgian state apparatus was a nightmare of a maze, but she did what she could and thought of the alternative had she not done so – unendurable poverty for many.

At ten past six she slapped a stamp on the last form in the

bottom file and dumped it in the out tray – ready for whoever was first into the office in the morning. Louise rose and stretched, a process that thrust out her considerable tummy so that it rested for a moment on the top of the desk. She glanced down, then considered the sight with sudden revulsion. The self-loathing thumped into her heart. Counter-productively her usual reaction to this was to seek comfort in cake. For once, though, the opposite happened. Her hunger vanished. She thought of Saskia's taut muscularity and winced. It was time for action.

It was also time for a drink, she decided. That this counter-manded the effectiveness of her first resolve was beside the point. She would not replace the cake with beer. She would re-place both with white wine. The real reduction in calories might not be substantial but anything that made her feel less so was a step in the right direction.

The Café Franck beckoned but Louise paused as she stepped out onto the pavement and looked out across the paved expanses of the Place Flagey. Last time she had crossed it she had lost her footing, her dignity and found a surprising lover at the same moment. Was she ready on this Monday evening for anything so adventurous again? Probably not. And her new revulsion at obesity precluded risking the stares of the trim Bohemians tasting their evening Prosecco at the Café Franck as well.

A survey of the alternatives to be had without leaving the square gave her a good handful of options.

She rejected the nice Lebanese café where Saskia had been dining before their fateful encounter. Louise needed more than Arab tea and, although she knew they did serve perfectly good wine and beer, suspected that for women that would only be acceptable with a meal, not for a lonely post-work snifter. The place further up on the right hand corner was too much of an eatery too and she wasn't in the mood for Guinness at the pseudo-Irish haunt close to the lake. That left the little traditional bar poking into the tramlines on the far side of the square. She made for it, not crossing the open space this time, but taking the long way round by the pavements that hugged the buildings. It meant crossing two more roads but after her misadventure on the Saturday she was less fearful of being hit by a car than by a hurtling Englishwoman.

Louise negotiated her way safely and pushed open the door of Le Pitch-pin. Nobody stared at her. The half dozen regulars looked as if most of them had been there all day and were passed caring anyway. Those that weren't gazing fixedly at the back of the bar or the racing column of Le Soir had their heads tilted to stare at the preliminaries to the evening's football on the big TV screen close to the ceiling.

The barmaid was a true barmaid: there all hours, figure on the brink of going to the dogs, looking older than she should, supremely indifferent to her customers unless they bought her a drink. She nodded to Louise and reached into the fridge for the white wine that the larger woman ordered. Louise immediately warmed to the place. No judgements here, it seemed to say; none of us is perfect, we are what we are. The glass of wine was bigger and cheaper than across the road in Café Frank too. She sipped it – and better!

It was hard to know where to sit in the small room. In the front window was too conspicuous, at the bar too much like asking for trouble or at least an invitation to talk and Louise wasn't ready for that either. The seats at the back of the room had the only group in them, four men in their sixties intent on a game of chess. That left just a table by the side window, facing into the room, or one just in front of the toilets.

She hovered.

The barmaid slid out from behind the counter and came towards her, waving a packet of cigarettes and collecting a glass of the same white wine on the way. She smiled at Louise.

'You smoke?'

'Yes,' said Louise instantly then stood in shock. She didn't smoke, never had. Why had she said yes? The companionship? Just because it felt right now, in this old bar? Because she wanted to fit in?

'Come on then,' said the barmaid and led the way to an outside pavement table.

No, it was none of those things, thought Louise, though nobody gave them a glance now that they were two women together with wine glasses. She was about to try smoking because a friend had lost five kilos in two weeks when she started. That was not to be coughed at.

~~~

A Germ Grows

The idea of reacting to the tiresome new constraints of traditional academic life by setting up a Free University was one that Fidel snorted at grumpily when Kathrin Deventer suggested it. What would a Free University look like anyway, he wondered? He glanced across the table in Café Franck at the beady-eyed and noncommittal face of his old friend and foe Hugo de Greef and decided the thought deserved contempt. It would soon look either like a salon for washed-up refusniks or, worse, one of those dreadful colleges springing up all over Brussels hoping to fleece foreign students with more money than sense and even less academic ability. Anything to get close to the honeyed corridors of the European Union.

He snorted again. Absurd.

A silence had come over the table. Fidel glanced around and saw to his surprise that everyone was staring at him, the English girl who was sitting with Patrice the barman with particular venom. Even Elise was looking frosty. What now? He hadn't said anything.

'You don't think he should have done?' the English girl Catrina asked with ice that went well beyond Elise's mild frost.

'Should have done what?' asked Fidel genuinely.

'Should have come to my rescue at least twice and made me happier in the last two days than at any time since I came to Belgium.'

'Who?'

'Patrice, of course,' Catrina said, laying a possessive and adoring hand on her lover's knee.

'I am pleased to hear it,'

'Then why did you snort like that?'

'Did I?'

'You did.' Hugo informed him, the twitch of an eye showing that he was enjoying his friend's discomfort a little more than was quite kind.

'It was not about you, my dear. I am afraid I was not listening very hard,' admitted Fidel.

'Then,' asked Elise, 'what were you snorting about?'

'This university thing.'

'The new one you are about to set up or the old one that is about to fire you?' Elise continued cruelly.

'Are they?'

'I don't know but you've been talking as if redecorating your office and getting fired are the same thing.'

'They are, very nearly. Making my conditions so abnormal and unfamiliar that I cannot teach, that I cannot engage with ideas, find the notations, the references I need, cannot...'

It was Elise's turn to snort. 'Just don't, darling, don't tell me you are an artist of the mind and that nobody understands the true conditions you require to propagate your great thoughts.'

'Well...'

'Don't.'

'Well I think it's a great idea – as long as it really is free to the students. Everything else that says it's free,' said Catrina with feeling, 'is free in every sense except for the people who actually need it to be.'

'So how would I get paid?' asked Fidel morosely as he considered a future without an institutional stipend, no office (redecorated or not) and coach loads of students clamouring outside his door for no reward.

It was the putative master in Modern Circus Studies who showed the mental agility to come up with an answer. 'Advertisers,' Elise announced.

'What will I be advertising? Would I put up posters around the room, wear a sponsored football shirt or endorse dog food on the metro?'

'Don't be silly, darling,' said Elise and leaned over to kiss him. Fidel thought this was very nice but a little demeaning and, while he had a lurking feeling that he was being made fun of, couldn't work out just how advertising was going to pay him to conduct off-campus sessions on political science.

Elise was not abashed. 'Why don't you and Patrice go and get more drinks while us creative ones design it all for you.'

It was just a little odd for the professor, notorious for his critical clarity, to find himself treated like a dotty aunt by a girl half his age – but then he remembered what Modern Circus Studies had taught him in bed for the last two nights and decided he might as well do as he was told for once. He and Patrice confirmed that everyone wanted the same again and toddled to the bar.

For a moment the three women all looked at the sagely Hugo for enlightenment but he was grinning sphinx-like at a far distant corner of the room and was clearly not going to invent anything just then. Perhaps a little mentoring further on but he was not inclined to produce ideas that he might actually have to put hours of labour into. So after a second the others ignored him and looked to each other for the next step.

'Are you serious?' asked Kathrin. 'Fidel may be right. How is he expected to find advertisers?'

Elise laughed. 'I've absolutely no idea,' she said. 'I just wanted him to think that if it was so easy that even I could figure it out then he must be a complete dinosaur not to be able to,'

'Was that fair?' asked Kathrin. Elise shrugged.

'You know,' Catrina said thoughtfully, 'it's not impossible.' The others looked at her expectantly. 'If he did it all online, like a televised masterclass, and we put the first one up on YouTube as a taster, then people could only get the rest of the sessions if they logged on with a password to a forum which carried advertising for books he mentioned, or other courses, it could work.'

Kathrin was being practical. 'Then you'll need a studio, someone to film the sessions, somebody to do the web design and hosting, a way of mediating the forum discussion...'

'Easy enough,' said Catrina, 'we do that sort of thing all the time at the Parliament. A lot of MEPs do online sessions with voters.'

Hugo was starting to look interested. 'Perhaps it need not be just Fidel giving seminars,' he mused. 'Perhaps I could use one of the organisations I am on the board of to administer the process and we really do make it a free online university.'

'Fine,' said Kathrin firmly, 'as long as that organisation is not mine.'

They paused as Fidel and Patrice reappeared from the bar carrying the round of drinks.

'Well?' asked Fidel once he had sat down. 'I suppose you have thought of a perfect solution.'

Elise sipped her white wine spritzer. 'Totally,' she said. 'All fixed. You can resign from your old university at the end of term.'

Flagey

IV

Tuesday

After Dinner

The first Esko knew that Tuesday was not going to be a usual day was when the phone rang in his office at 10am and he was asked if he would like to comment to Le Soir?

'Comment on what?'

'Oh come come, M. Nystrom, surely I don't have to explain?'

'I'm afraid you do.'

'Then you have not seen the photograph in this morning's Bonjour!?'

Esko thought he was on safe ground and anyway he assumed that any photograph on which he was being asked to comment was likely either to be of his party leader or his wife and the answer to both would be the same. Non.

'I regret Bonjour! is not a journal I take, either in the office or at home,' he replied as primly as he could.

'Well, M. Nystrom, on this occasion I suggest you do. Perhaps I will ring you back in half an hour?'

'Perhaps you will but perhaps I will not be available.'

'We shall see,' and the gruff wheedling voice of the journalist cut off.

Esko was disinclined to rush to the ground floor where the newspaper and souvenir shop nestled alongside the bank in the parliamentary shopping plaza. It was bound to be some speculative story about either the party's connections to disreputable businessmen, or possibly Rikka caught slipping out of one of the flimsy dresses she had taken to wearing recently now that her star status was rising.

The only thing that puzzled him was why that should have made it into the Belgian papers, rather than the Finnish ones – unless, of course she had swapped him for a Belgian politician which, even in his gloomiest moments, Esko could not imagine. He shrugged and turned his mind back to memories of Amelie and then, more prosaically, to the voting sheet for the morning's plenary session. This looked a bit odd. According to his diligent reading of the day before the party seemed to have reversed its position on almost every amendment.

A few minutes later he was left in no doubt what the call had been about when Roberto Vincenzi, the ebullient leader of his group and of the Italian Republican Social Liberals (RSL for short) bubbled through the doorway.

'You are a lucky boy!' he began, brandishing a copy of the aforementioned news rag in front of him like football flag.

'Why, exactly?' asked the mystified Esko.

'What do you mean, why?' chuckled Roberto. 'What some of us would give to be in your shoes or...,' he leered, 'your trousers more particularly.'

Esko took the paper, opened at page five, from his leader's hands. The photograph was rather beautiful and romantic, if you excluded the fact that it was of Esko himself and Amelie, locked in a kiss as he helped her button her coat against the warm red wallpaper of the hall of Lucio's expensively fashionable restaurant the night before. The lips gave away the fact that this was not a strictly average kiss between acquaintances, a point made explicit by a sub picture of the two of them, hand in hand, entering the doorway of Esko's apartment building with the caption '...and later'.

'Ah,' said Esko, flopping back in his seat.

The grin on Roberto's face verged on the revolting. 'You and Amelie Poitiers, I mean how do you do it?'

'Thank you for alerting me, Roberto. It is certainly unfortunate.'

'Not at all. The party needs all the glamour we can get. It will do wonders for our reputation – and yours, naturally.'

The Finn stood up from his desk, laid down the newspaper and gently but firmly guided the Italian out of the office. 'Not quite that simple, I'm afraid,' he said, and locked the door in his leader's face.

He sank down with his head in his hands on the sofa before reaching into his top pocket for the mobile phone. He hoped

Amelie was still in bed and had not stood at his window naked, nor responded to the doorbell.

The phone was answered on its second ring. 'I know,' Amelie said before he had even identified himself. 'I'm so sorry.'

'Sorry?'

'I thought we had been so careful but obviously not careful enough. It will be hard for you, a politician?'

'Yes and no. Don't worry about me. But how did you find out? Are you still at my place?'

'I am. My agent texted me and sent the picture to my phone half an hour ago. I was too embarrassed to ring you. And the doorbell has been ringing every ten minutes. My agent says I am not to answer it or look out of the window.'

'He's right, I expect. The vultures will be gathering.'

'Are you angry?'

Esko paused. How did he feel, he wondered? 'With them, yes. I hate it. With you? Absolutely not. Being pictured with you makes me very proud indeed. And I meant every pixel of that kiss.'

'You did?' Amelie giggled and then turned serious, 'but you are married.'

'It seems so. But I rather wonder for how long. I wouldn't be surprised if this is just the excuse Rikka is looking for – and it means she can pretend she is not the one with the lover.'

'Isn't she?'

'I don't know, not for sure.'

'I'm sorry.'

'So you keep saying, Amelie. But don't be, at least not yet.'

They were silent to each other for a moment.

'What shall I do?' Amelie asked eventually. 'I am meant to do this stupid chat show on TV this evening. Now they will talk of nothing else. Maybe I should cancel but I don't know that I can. It's in my contract for the film publicity. Maybe my agent could make them agree not to talk about the picture?'

'That would never work. They'll find a way to mention it, even if they've agreed in theory. You would just look foolish.'

'So...?'

Esko thought quickly. 'Can you wait there – just until my voting is over at one o'clock?'

'Sure.'

'Good. Don't move. I'm not letting you leave there alone.'

Perhaps the worst part of the rest of the morning was not the furious call from political PR managers in Finland, nor the hurt and meaningful glances from his assistant Mariana as she brought in a pile of email printouts after refusing to put through the follow-up call from Le Soir, but the digs in the ribs and knowing pats on the back from fellow members, whatever their party or gender, as he made his way into the debating chamber an hour later.

Somewhere along the way he had lost the voting sheet Mariana had prepared for him and so just voted the way he felt right or abstained if he wasn't bothered. He didn't know it yet but the morning's inaction was the making of his political career.

~~~

Vultures Waiting

It was not unusual to see TV crews in Café Franck; after all, the building had been built as the headquarters for French Belgian television back in the thirties and it still housed a couple of production companies and a community station with small studios. It was unusual, though, to see a clutch of them - and strangers to the café at that. When Mercedes pushed into the bar for an early lunch of tuna salad on Tuesday she could barely get to the food counter for the men in fur-lined parkas and over made-up women reporters standing around piles of steel edged cases. She had noticed that there were white vans with the tell-tale satellite dishes on the roof parked around the lake.

Was it, she wondered, just preparation for one of the endless EU ceremonies that seemed to be gradually taking over the building on a regular basis? In which case lunch was likely to be interrupted soon by motorcades of screaming sirens and flashing blue lights.

The demeanour of the crews suggested that was not the case, though, and Mercedes knew Brussels well enough to know that only big EU events were ever likely to attract media attention on this scale at Tuesday lunchtime. Maybe there was a body in the lake? She shuddered at the thought. But that would have attracted a massive circus of police vans and scene of crime tape too and there was none of that that she could see. The crews looked as though they had been there all morning, were bored to tears and badly needed a beer. Every now and then one of them would gaze through the window, across the lake, towards an apartment block on the far shore where, she noticed as she grabbed an obscure table towards the back of the café, another clutch of media types were milling around.

Mercedes was half way through her uninspiring mess of tuna and green beans, served equally uninspiringly in a thick glass jar, when she was asked politely in French thickened by a rich Eastern European accent whether the other seat was taken. She looked up, mid green bean, and smiled. She recognised the new arrival as Nikita, who ran or owned (Mercedes was never quite sure which) a small art gallery showing ferocious semi-abstract paintings halfway up the hill towards Avenue Louise. Mercedes was on the mailing list for the private views, more for the free vin mousseux and the vaguely interesting company she met there than for the paintings, if truth be told.

'Of course.'

Nikita had all the trappings of the Russian grande-dame, though she cannot have been much more than thirty in reality. He blonde hair was always piled high on her head, her eyebrows plucked within a millimetre of existence and then heavily outlined again in black. She favoured voluminous grey tops (silk in summer, wool in winter) that suggested a full figure without ever quite revealing the reality. Her waist was tiny, though, and she made sure she wore black trousers tight enough to make it abundantly clear. She had indeed been born Russian, although from the farther southern reaches of the Ukraine than from within the modern borders, and she knew well enough that her air of exotic sophistication sold rather more paintings to her clients than their natural appreciation of contemporary art.

She placed her cappuccino and a similar tuna salad to Mercedes' on the table and looked around her with distaste.

'I never normally come here for lunch,' Nikita said, 'but my usual place across from the gallery is full of these people too, so I thought I might find more space down here. Evidently not. What about you?'

For Mercedes the Café Franck had been almost a second home until the frightful Dutchwoman had doused her with boiling tea the previous Saturday. This lunch was the first time she had ventured in since but Nikita did not need to know all that.

'Yes, I'm here often. The food's terrible but the place suits me.'

The two women paused to take mouthfuls of tuna and olive.

'Who are these people anyway?' asked Mercedes. 'What are they are doing here now?'

'Oh it is so silly,' Nikita dismissed them with a wave of her hand. 'There was a picture in the paper this morning. Some French actress who had been at the film festival here kissing one of those European Parliament people at Lucio's last night. He lives across the lake there, or so one of this lot told me.'

'All this for a kiss?'

'Ridiculous, isn't it! But then I read it so thousands of others did too. Politician kisses film star makes better news than economic crisis and another Arab war, I suppose.'

'Poor woman. I would hate to have my life shown like this.'

Nikita shrugged. 'She's an actress. She probably organised it.'

Across the lake the actress who had 'probably organised it' was lying in bed with her head under the duvet in the hope that it would muffle the insistent alternate ringing of the doorbell and her mobile phone.

She was contemplating whether she could keep far enough out of sight of the windows to have a shower. There were curtains at the front of the flat and in the bedroom, but not in the kitchen at the back, and the bathroom was across a landing that was exposed to the rear view, so to speak; not an issue in normal life but a hell of a risk when there were paparazzi about with long lenses and full wallets for bribing the neighbours.

Perhaps she should just get drunk. Instead Amelie sobbed quietly and waited for Esko to return from Parliament. She hoped he would have rather more idea of what to do next than she had.

~~~

Stirring It

On Tuesday lunchtime Catrina stood at the end of the lunch queue and scanned the Parliamentary canteen for a place to park herself once she had filled the tray. There were not many spaces free. She was not surprised to see fellow MEP's assistant Mariana sniffling alone in a corner. It had often struck her that the neurotic Finn was the sort of girl that sniffled – either from imaginary allergies or equally fantasised emotional torment. Catrina paid for a chicken escalope, sautéed potatoes and haricot beans – opted for rosé instead of bottled water and looked for somewhere else to sit. There was nowhere that was not a solitary place among a close-knit group where she would either be clearly intruding or have no hope of one of her own friends joining her.

Resignedly she made her way across the cheerless room

between the functional white tables to Mariana. 'May I join you?' she asked briskly and sat down, ignoring both the potential reply and the sniffles.

Mariana paused in the act of blowing her nose and looked guardedly at the English girl who had seemed so keen to avoid her only a few days earlier. Not that she cared. She had new issues to worry about and the return of that thought brought back the welling of tears and the urge to howl.

Her companion opened her wine, poured and tasted it, and cut herself a slab of escalope before allowing herself to notice the Finn's distress. With the first edge of hunger blunted, though, she smiled breezily.

'What's up?'

Mariana looked at her without comprehension. 'I mean,' Catrina began again, despairing at the formality of Euro English, 'what's been happening to you today?'

There was no spoken answer. Instead Mariana produced the offending edition of Bonjour! from under the table and plonked it, open at the photo of Esko and Amelie, on the table beside Catrina's plate. Catrina lifted a fork full of potato and glanced at the paper without much interest until she recognised Esko and read the picture caption.

'Ooh!' she exclaimed, impressed, and not a little pleased that someone she vaguely knew was in the papers, 'who'd have thought it. Clever him!'

It was not the reaction Mariana was looking for. The tears came, she grabbed the paper, pushed backed her chair and stalked off with uttering another word.

Catrina shrugged, then giggled quietly as she went on with lunch. Honestly, what was wrong with that woman, she asked herself. No sense of humour or fun. You'd think she'd be proud in a dodgy sort of way of working for a member with such exquisite and glamorous taste in mistresses. And he was a hell of a lot nicer than the slug Catrina worked for. Then the realisation hit her. Mariana was in love with Esko herself and suddenly he was even more out of reach than the mere fact of marriage made him. Poor kid. Really, Catrina should have thought of that before she opened her mouth.

'Of course!' she said out loud to her glass of rosé.

'Of course, what?'

She looked up with fork halfway to her face and her spirits took an instant dive.

'May I sit down?'

She allowed her mouth to go through a full round of chewing as she looked icily at the new arrival.

'Nothing's reserved in here,' she answered without enthusiasm.

Bruno! She wondered how he had the nerve or even the will to speak to her as the tweed-suited young man with slicked blond hair lowered himself into the seat Mariana had vacated. Until the previous weekend and her discovery of Patrice she had been nursing the contradictory emotions of fury at having been dumped by the young Tory from somewhere in Surrey and fury at herself for ever having taken up with someone she instinctively disliked so much in the first place.

'So, of course what?' Bruno asked in his especially irritating habit of beginning a conversation without preliminaries, as if they had been together all day instead of not being on speaking terms for three weeks.

'Good afternoon, Bruno. How are you?' countered Catrina frostily, deliberately filling in the pleasantries that Bruno had ignored.

'Fine thanks. Think I'm going to get that Phd place at St. Andrews, you know.'

Catrina ignored that information too, storing up the quip it deserved till later. 'Found anybody to show your newt collection to?'

Bruno was instantly stung. 'Fishing flies and you know it,' he protested.

'The things you carry around in your trousers, are they?' Schoolgirl smut was not usually Catrina's habit but there were times when nothing else would do.

'Well, if you're going to be like that...' Bruno huffed and, picking up his tray, moved to another table that had come free on the other side of the room.

The rosé had done her a real favour, Catrina decided as she finished the dregs and the chicken. She felt a little unlike herself though. It was not often, actually she could not remember a time ever, when she had successfully driven away two people from a lunch table in the space of ten minutes.

After leaving the canteen she impulsively diverted from the path that would have taken her to the lifts in E tower, where her boss had his office, and took the escalator to the third floor concourse that is the crossing point between all the different sectors of the European Parliament building. She pushed her way to the front of the crush at the coffee bar and waited her turn, long in coming as the flurry of lobbyists, assistants and members tried to grab caffeine before the afternoon sessions and meetings began.

She found herself jammed against a woman she recognised as Gwynneth Price, the Welsh Nationalist member only a decade older than herself who sat with the Green Group in the chamber. Emboldened by the wine, she spoke.

'Hi, sorry to try this...'

'Hello,' said the MEP warily.

'I'm Catrina. I work for Roger Belstead.'

The Welsh woman grimaced. 'Poor you.'

'Yes. It's frightful. He's a slug.'

'He is too,' Gwynneth Price looked at the girl next to her properly for the first time. 'But why tell me?'

Catrina gulped. It was all so unplanned. 'Just now, seeing you here,' she gulped again, 'I thought, I mean I wondered whether you need anybody, you know, with a bit of experience here?'

'You mean you want to swap him for me.'

'Oh yes.' Catriona just had time to say before the attendant demanded her order.'

Gwynneth smiled. 'Let's take this coffee over there and talk about it.'

~~~

Dropping The Drawbridge

On most days Esko never went back from Parliament to his flat by Flagey at lunchtime. There was no need and there was never a let-up between meetings. But that particular autumn Tuesday was different. There was a beautiful French actress besieged on the second floor of his apartment building - besieged by cameramen and reporters as effectively as if she had been a mediaeval princess stuck in a tower while the forces of the Duke of Burgundy prowled about on the other side of the moat.

Had Esko been in the habit of going home for lunch, he would normally have climbed onto a 38 or a 54 bus, as he did most mornings on the way into the office. He would not have claimed his right and booked himself a car from the parliamentary drivers' pool, which in theory were only to be used between functions and the airport, or exceptionally, going home after a full day of both.

For once, though, it was a right that needed to be exercised and slightly abused. He didn't bother Mariana, his one fit assistant, which was lucky, given her mood. Even if she had been in splendid form, being an earnest young Finn, she would have pursed her lips in puritanical disapproval. Esko stopped off at the transport office on his way down to the hemicycle for the late morning vote and put in his request.

The moment the last red button had been pushed an hour later, signalling his rejection of motions put forward by the European People's Party, he scurried from his seat and, evading the wisecracks of his colleagues, hared down the escalators without waiting for the more sociable lifts.

Once swinging through the back streets of Ixelles, Esko straightened his hair and tie, girded the belt of his trousers and urged his brain into warrior mode. He warned the driver that there was likely to be trouble the other end but that, whatever the obstructions, he was not to stop until he was right by the kerb in front of the door. He was then to come round and open Esko's passenger door to give him some burly protection from the swarming hacks.

'Are you going back to the Parliament? Do you want me to wait?'

'Can you?'

'I'm not meant to, but I will,' said the driver, grinning as he looked in his mirror. 'Here's my phone number. I'll wait round the corner. Just give me a call when you're ready – unless you are going to be in there all afternoon.'

'No, half an hour at most. Do you mind?'

'Not at all – a lot more fun than the usual job.'

There was a pause as they negotiated their way round a parked bus on Rue Malibran. Esko frowned. So the driver knew more than he was saying.

As they moved forward in a straight line again the driver asked, 'Is she as nice as she looks in the pictures?'

'Ah, you know.'

The driver shrugged, 'I read,' he said, tapping the newspaper on the seat next to him.

Esko slumped back against the armrest. 'I think so. But you can judge for yourself. You may be meeting her soon.'

As they drove out into the open square of Flagey and saw the encampment of TV vans on the other side, the driver laughed.

'Sir, you are big news today!

Esko swore.

The driver laughed again. 'No problem. We fix them. I am from Albania. We know how to do this.'

'I hope so, but no fighting the press,' Esko warned, thoroughly alarmed at thought of the headline 'Parliament Driver Punches Cameraman'.

'OK, OK.' There was clear disappointment in his new minder's voice. Just to prove the point he accelerated, rather than slowed, as he turned round the lake and headed for the media knot gathered on the doorstep.

It was a smart tactic because the speed at which he swerved

to the kerb had reporters jumping to the pavement before they could prepare themselves for Esko's arrival. Seemingly in one movement the Albanian driver had stopped, got out, pushed his way round to the other side of the car, and swung open the passenger door.

The surprise worked and, ready with his magnetic key, Esko was out of the car and into the apartment building with the door slammed by the time the startled reporters had pulled their microphones out and the cameramen found the focus. All they had to film was the back of a man in a grey suit pushing a door. There was consternation and a frenzied ringing of entry phone bells but by then all the residents in the building had learnt to ignore them for the day.

Esko slipped upstairs and unlocked his door. He pushed. It gave a centimetre or two then stopped. Amelie was either dead behind it or taking precautions.

'Amelie – it's me,' Esko called out softly.

An eye appeared at the crack. There was a judder as furniture was pulled back just enough for Esko to squeeze through. Grinning, he slammed the door and pushed back the restraining sofa before gathering Amelie in the tightest hug he could muster. It was only halfway through that he realised she was still naked.

'Darling,' Amelie whispered into his ear, 'if I don't get to the bathroom soon there is going to be a disaster, so before we get any further could you please shut the kitchen door so I can get there without windows. My clothes are in there.'

'Of course,' but Esko was puzzled, 'but all the reporters are out at the front.'

'And the photographers? Don't you believe it.'

Esko moved as fast as he could out of the clinch and to the kitchen, where he closed the door and started to make coffee as nonchalantly as possible while Amelie shut herself gratefully into the secure and unobservable bathroom. It was likely to be more than a token visit before she was ready to face her new lover, the press or the world at large.

~ ~ ~

Significant Encounters

'The answer is yes, I do need a new assistant, and soon,' Gwynneth Price admitted as they sat in the coffee bar on the concourse of the European Parliament. Catrina beamed. 'But,' the MEP continued, 'don't get your hopes up just yet.'

Catrina's beam melted away. 'Oh.'

'Where are you from?'

'Derby,' the younger woman confessed, as though that alone would make her unemployable.

'So speaking Welsh is not likely to be on your CV.' It was a statement, not a question.

'I'm afraid not.'

'Pity. And therefore dealing with all matters Welsh for a

Welsh Nationalist is going to be tough for you.' There was a glint, though, in Gwynneth's eye as she asked, 'and how are you on the thought and works of Saunders Lewis? Where do you stand on the Daffydd Ellis Thomas question and the continuance of the monarchy?'

'Um....'

'Yes, I can see we agree, though don't you dare say that to anybody else around here.'

There was a lull while Catrina sipped her black coffee and stared into its fathomless dark.

'No chance, then?'

'You mean, am I going to abandon you to the political halitosis of Roger Belstead? I don't think that would be fair and anyway you might be part of the solution. How's your French?'

Catrina took a deep breath and launched into a quick francophone description of what she thought of her current boss and all his party that would have shocked the Daily Telegraph to its core.

'That'll do nicely,' grinned Gwynneth. 'Better than mine, which is the important thing. The problem I have is that I get plenty of people applying who know everything about the intricacies of fratricide in Wales and the implications of local dialects. If I was a member of the Welsh Assembly that would be vital. But I'm not. I'm a member of the Green Group here, which is led by the French and is about as interested in the cultural correctness of Wales as I am of Savoy. What I need is an assistant to carry credibility with them but who is equally not French and can get along with the English Greens too. Do you think you can do that?'

For a moment Catrina was wracked by doubt. Being Belstead's little helpmate was depressing but it was also simple enough. She was neither expected nor encouraged to have opinions; just to answer the phone in a middle-class, middle-England, voice and précis the continuous stream of documents that flowed into any MEP's inbox. If she moved into Gwynneth Price's office she would have to think, substitute at meetings, at least make a stab a guessing what the right course of action was going to be.

The woman from Wales was, she realised, offering her a proper grown-up job. The question was real. Did she think she could do that?

Her father's no-nonsense engineer's clarity took over in her head for an instant and she felt herself smile, heard herself say, 'I'm sure I can.'

'Good,' said Gwynneth, draining her coffee cup and getting to her feet. 'Give me your private mobile number, print out a copy of your CV – don't email it, bring it round to my office later, then we'll get serious.'

Catrina sat on, watching the incessant stream of parliamentarians, assistants, those demanding their attention as journalists or advocates, the purposeful flow of political humanity each convinced that their next action, their fragment of detail, would somehow make the world a better place. Occasionally, but much more occasionally than they liked to think, they were right and the world (or parts of it) took a little lurch towards civilisation. Mostly, though, even the grandest resolutions went unnoticed and uncared for.

Perhaps that was not the point. Without the detritus and accumulated mediocrity of bad art there would be no good art. Without the pointless barrage of irrelevant politics, there would be no important politics.

Which was all very well, thought Catrina, as she made her way to distant lifts, but she would still far rather work for someone who had views that she at least half agreed with. Belstead or Price. There was no competition.

Up in the Tory member's office there was no sound at all. A text on the phone she had left on her desk told her that Belstead had 'been required in London suddenly' and had disappeared the moment the morning's voting session closed. That probably meant, Catrina reflected, that one or other of his vile children had been arrested for cocaine possession again, or that Newsnight were so desperate for infantile views on Europe that only Belstead would be inane enough.

If Belstead was gone, Catrina knew, his other office lapdogs fresh from Eton and Oxford would have gone too and would now be on their third carafe of something expensive at the pavement tables of Place Luxembourg. All of which suited her very well. Normally she would have been stalking round the office swearing at the sheer presumption that she, as the only female and only one old enough to drink in some American states, could take care of everything.

Her last vestige of interest in Belstead and his world had evaporated, though.

She ignored the urgent emails and settled down to revise the story of her life as she intended to present it later that afternoon. The process was not long for neither, she was moderately depressed to realise, was the story. Looking at the page and a half of biographical statement her progress through the world had seemed to be unremarkable. Yet behind every bald fact and job description there was a richer reality and if, she allowed herself to dream as the printer burbled out, she could swap E tower for G tower in this vast building, reality could become richer still. In the course of five days she would have transformed the two most important aspects of her life; how she spent her days and how she spent her nights. And, vitally, who with.

~~~

Together And Not Together

Just as Esko was zipping up Amelie's dress his wife rang. The tabloid sensation of the day in Belgium had clearly found it's way to Finland, judging from the silence at the other end of the phone. Esko would have thought it was just an ill-timed marketing sell had the arctic frost from the other end not transmitted itself so stringently, giving an all-together different sense to the phrase cold calling.

The first words down the line were clear enough, though. 'Esko, you should know that I'm leaving you. From now.'

If it was a shock move, meant to throw Esko into a paroxysm of indecision, a desperate lurch from the woman dressing beside him to the one making her announcement from Helsinki, then it was a miscalculated one. Clearly Esko was expected to start making some excuses, plead his cause, tell Amelie there and then that she meant nothing, that a Finnish political dynasty depended on his abject apology.

Had she called on Saturday, when Esko was morosely sitting in Café Franck being surly with his assistant and doodling Rikka's name with longing, he would have been shaken to his socks. She had not called, though, not once since he had returned from Finland earlier in the month.

Instead Esko found he had not felt so calm for weeks. He just said, 'I know. Of course you are. Why don't you put the details in writing,' closed his phone and threw it across the room into a heap of clothes.

Amelie looked round and frowned. 'Who was that?'

'Rikka, my wife. She's seen the pictures. She's leaving me.'

'Oh Esko, I'm so sorry. It's all my fault.'

'No it's not. I didn't have to kiss you in the street. And

anyway, I think it's just brought forward her decision.'

'Why?'

'She's bored. More ambitious than me and tired of having an older lover who is not as impressed with her political infallibility as she wants. She's found someone who fits her new fame better.'

'I'm sorry,' said Amelie again.

'Two days ago I was too. Now I don't care. I've found you and all the pain has gone away.'

Amelie turned and kissed him: a very different kiss from either their love-making or the desperate greeting as he had come through the door earlier.

'It seems so.'

There was a silence, or there was between them. Outside a police siren was speeding closer and the doorbell started ringing. Inside, so did all their phones.

Esko's shoulders drooped. 'Should we look?'

'I suppose we should.'

They broke like a pair of wrestlers retreating to their corners and hunted through clothes and bags for mobiles. Esko's was found first. He ignored the voicemails, the emails and the missed calls. The texts were mostly predictable but then, accidentally touching the screen icon for twitter, he discovered what all the fuss was about. Rikka had done as she was told and put it all in writing: not to his lawyers, as Esko had intended, but to the world – via Twitter.

'Rat husband likes French bimbo better. Good luck Esko. Leaving now. #rikka#finnpolleft'

Esko guffawed and handed the phone to Amelie. 'Oh dear,' she said.

'It is accurate at least,' he said with a grin, then realised that would not be quite good enough, 'all except the word bimbo, of course.'

'Of course,' Amelie jabbed him fiercely in the ribs, 'and make sure you remember it.'

They switched off their phones again and perched side by side on the bed. After a moment Esko stood up and strolled into the kitchen and returned with two glasses and a bottle of champagne. 'Would this help?'

'It could.'

He uncorked and poured. She sipped. 'You have good taste, at least in champagne.'

'Would it have been the end if I hadn't?'

She met his eyes severely. 'Definitely. The end.'

Esko gulped half his glass then said quietly, 'If it is not the end, what is it?'

'Half the world's press seem to be outside your door asking the same question.'

Esko topped up her glass. 'It's too late for the beginning. We seem to have begun in a way that makes today a very long way from last Tuesday.'

It was Amelie's turn to take half her champagne in one. 'Then we must make plans for the rest of the week, I think.'

'Seriously?'

She pressed his hand. 'Seriously.'

For the next five minutes they discussed what that could mean, where they might go. Neither, they admitted, could afford to ignore their diaries completely until Thursday, at least not if they wanted a career on Friday.

They drank more of the champagne. Esko, they decided, would maintain a dignified silence, issuing a simple statement through his office in Helsinki, only in Finnish, announcing his sadness at the separation from his wife and his continuing support for her political future. He would not mention Amelie at all in that but they would talk to reporters on the doorstep.

Amelie, though, would play the film star to the hilt, appear on as many TV shows as her agent and producers wanted before Friday, then call a halt. She would coyly argue, quietly truthfully up to a point, that she and Esko had only just met, were just good friends, and that anything else was too early to tell.

Once the champagne was finished and, just to steady themselves, they had raided the kitchen for a sandwich so that they wouldn't trip into the arms of the reporters, Esko called the Parliamentary driver who had brought him home.

'Sorry boss,' he answered, 'I couldn't wait any longer. I'm back in the garage. I sent you three messages and a voicemail. Guess you were busy,' he chortled.

'Oh,' Esko was thrown for a second, 'I suppose I can try a taxi.'

'No, no, boss. I can be with you. 15 minutes. No problem.'

Esko relayed the answer to Amelie, who nodded. 'OK, thank you.'

'A bit of a wait. What shall we do?'

Amelie touched his lips with her fingers. 'I'm going to have a little tweet and then make myself up to look like a film star again. Watch.'

The message on Twitter was the work of a true pro.

'Made a good friend this weekend. You all seem to know that already. Just wait. No news is good news.

~~~

Right Place, Wrong Move

By nine o'clock on Tuesday evening Café Franck was getting loud and the crowd was a lot younger than it had been at lunchtime, or in the genteel part of the morning when café normal and thé de menthe was the general order. Mercedes was back, though, dressed smartly because her potential consort for the evening was also likely to be smart, being Italian, and the possibility of a change of job beckoned if she played her cards right. She bought herself a small beer and waited by the window looking out over the lake.

On the other side of the café she watched an avuncular middle-aged man, rather red in the face, trying hard and failing to charm a much younger woman by attempting to look as if he belonged, which at this time of night in Café Franck and with the music this loud, he clearly didn't. Mercedes couldn't see the woman's face but that didn't matter. What had struck her with instant jealousy was the woman's mass of black hair, cascading in curly waves passed her shoulders. No wonder the old boy was smitten.

Mercedes instinctively patted her own neat short straight black stuff, which shone but never cascaded. It was doubly unfair that at the adjacent table an even younger girl had an almost matching flow of hair so subtly blonde it was almost impossible to decide whether it was tinged with red or brown.

This was Agnestina, nineteen, student of French literature who, in her first month at university, was just beginning to wonder whether there might be something beyond tolerant friendship with the gauche boy who sat across the table.

And boy was the only way to describe him, though they were the same age to within a few weeks. He was thin, had hair a little longer than the fasion, admittedly only a shade darker than her own, but self consciously swept across his brow like a bald man does to hide his patch. He wore a sandy round neck pullover and kept pulling at the sleeve – a sign of nerves, she wondered, or just an annoying habit?

There was much that was absurd about him. For a start he was called Flamand and anybody less flammable or flaming she had never met. He talked about wanting to be a poet and she dreaded the moment when, as he inevitably would, he slipped a well thumbed little notebook onto the table and offered to read. On the other hand he was beautiful, there was no denying, in that soppy way that Elves in Tolkien were beautiful, and he did peer at her with the sweetest lovesick blue-grey eyes as she babbled on about her discovery of Maupassant.

Over at the bar Elise was having a spot of bother. There was no show at the theatre up the road on Tuesdays so she was doing an extra shift in Café Franck. The long side of the L-shape was being looked after by two of her male colleagues, neither of whom she knew particularly well, but who seemed to have worked together enough to have found a steady rhythm which did not need her.

That left Elise with the short side. The trouble was that four stools had been placed there. The two nearest the kitchen and toilet doors didn't matter too much because nobody usually ordered from there anyway. However the two others were in prime position. It was impossible, if they were occupied, for anybody needing a drink to get to the bar and just at the moment they were occupied so effectively they might have been the taken by the Wehrmacht in 1942.

The queue behind was becoming querulous.

The occupants couldn't have cared less. A slightly exotic woman, perhaps with a touch of India or the near east, in her early thirties, was being kissed as though she needed continuous resuscitation by a bearded bespectacled man of similar age with a canvas bag slung from his shoulders. His concentration on his task was total. She was compliant though not quite as enthusiastic and, when she opened her eyes briefly and caught Elise's glare, she did her best to disengage. Bearded wonder was having none of it, though, and redoubled the ferocity of his clinch. As Elise tried to reach round to pass a drink to her exasperated clients he pulled back to take a breath, nearly knocking the full beer from her hand.

She'd had enough. She tapped him smartly on the shoulder. No reaction. He'd plunged in for a new session.

Elise reached beneath the bar for an empty bottle and a spoon. She held the bottle close to the beard and began to bang it fiercely. Nothing doing. In front of her the leading drink seekers applauded appreciatively at her efforts but still the grappling continued.

Clearly desperate measures were needed. Either she could get the others behind the bar to evict the lovers, though they were busy too and she knew it would just mean that she would be teased for the rest of the evening, or she could take matters into her own hands.

She reached beneath the bar again and this time came up with a handful of ice. The beard was likely to be oblivious but his exotic companion had her hair draped forward from her neck, leaving the back of her shirt exposed. Elise slipped the ice smartly into the collar.

There was a shriek and the woman shot upright, butting the beard so that he bit his tongue sharply. Finally, as he clutched his mouth and the queue looked on in awe, Elise had their attention.

'Thank you,' she began. 'This is a bar, not a bedroom. If you wish to make love here you can do so on the seats in the corner over there,' she pointed to the right, 'by the window. Otherwise, go home or find a hotel. Either way, go away.'

The beard was about to protest but two things stopped him. One was the cheering from all the thirsty people surrounding him, another was his amour's giggles as she faced Elise, whispered 'thank you' back and, collecting her coat, fled into the night.

Meanwhile Mercedes' interviewer had arrived: a dapper Italian in a tight grey suit and expansively knotted red tie. He spotted Mercedes, saw that she had half a beer, bought himself a whisky with a lot of ice, and joined her.

Flagey

V

Wednesday

A Busy Morning

Catrina woke in rather a daze on Wednesday morning. She reached across, hoping to come across the comforting form of Patrice to snuggle up against but then remembered with the first sigh of the day that he was not there. He hadn't actually moved in and anyway he had sent a text message explaining that he was on the early 'coffee and croissant' shift at Café Franck.

The longer she lay struggling into wakefulness the more dazed Catrina seemed to become. She was not good at mornings at the best of times. Had she really approached a Plaid Cymru MEP the day before and demanded to work for her? Had she really had the courage to walk out of the office at 3pm just because all the men in the pay of the awful Roger Belstead hadn't come back from lunch on time? She drew the duvet around her shoulders more tightly and tried to get back to dreaming. There was no denying, though. She had done both things. What with coming together for a helluva lot more than an occasional glass of rosé with Patrice too, the last four days had been revolutionary. She had even been stratospherically rude to the erstwhile slob-cum-boyfriend Bruno. Catrina wondered whether it meant she was growing up at last or whether there was something weird going on with the cycle of her period.

Who cared, she decided, as she tottered in her t-shirt and check flannel pyjama bottoms to the micro-kitchen and switched the kettle on for tea. Stuff'em, she decided as she stripped in the bathroom: all except Patrice, of course.

By the time she arrived in the office her resolution was restored. It was reinforced further by the sight of still empty desks. Clearly her ingenue fellow toilers for Belstead had followed an indefinite lunch with an indeterminate night in the clubs.

Catrina looked with fresh disdain at the tin trunk waiting in the corridor for all the indispensable documents that needed to be shipped down to Strasbourg for the following week's plenary session. Belstead hadn't read them, she hadn't read them and she very much doubted if anybody else had either, apart from the Group Co-ordinator who had to decide how Belstead and his like-minded slugs were meant to vote.

With her usual inability to take little decisions, Catrina stood in the middle of the room trying to work out whether to make a coffee in the expensive but hopeless machine Belstead had been given as a kick back for blocking a clause against the exploitation of plantation workers by multinationals, retracing her steps to the counters on level 3, or just settling down and switching on the computer.

She sat down and switched on, more because it gave her time to work through the coffee options than out of any enthusiasm for what she might find in her inbox. She had barely logged on when her mobile rang.

'Catrina?'

'Yes.'

'Gwynneth. Are you busy?'

'No. Nobody else is in yet.'

'Lazy bastards, but knowing Belstead why am I not surprised? Can you meet me downstairs in ten minutes, same place we met yesterday?'

'Yes, of course.'

Well, she thought with a grin, that solved that.

A few seconds later the door crashed open and Belstead's two juniors, Peregrine and Nigel, lurched giggling into the room. Catrina glanced up from her computer and shuffled some paper as if she had been there for hours, if not all night.

'Do I know you?' she began. 'Oh yes, you were the two who were meant to start work here about two months ago.'

'Oh don't be a cat, Cat,' Peregrine sniggered. 'Nobody will have missed us.'

Catrina fixed him with the most superior glare she could muster. 'You have no idea just how true that is.'

She could act fifty when she wanted, she reflected, as Peregrine plonked himself down at the other side of the desk. Nigel merely slumped. His shade of greeny grey told who had come off worse from the night.

'Now you're here,' continued Catrina, 'you can take over the correspondence emails. I'm going to pick up the post. Won't be long.' And she strode out with the majesty of a matron.

There was more trepidation in her step as she walked past the MEPs' pigeon holes on level 3 to the coffee bar. She was about to go and order when she spotted Gwynneth Price at one of the small corner tables. The Welshwoman waved her over.

'I got you a cappuccino. I hope that's what you like?'

'Always,' which was not quite true but Catrina was glad to have the matter taken out of her hands.

'I looked at your CV.'

Catrina wondered if she was meant to respond and was furious when she heard herself come out with, 'it's nothing special, I'm afraid.'

'Possibly not,' Gwynneth smiled.

Damn, thought Catrina. I knew it. Back to Belstead.

'But,' the MEP went on, 'I think we can fix that. Anyway, you're who I want.'

Clouds lifted and a choir seemed to be singing great chunks of Handel. 'You do?'

'I do. Now, how quickly can you change over?'

The clouds lowered a fraction. 'Um, I've no idea.'

'Do you have a contract?'

'Not exactly,' admitted Catrina, 'unless the letter offering me the job counts.'

'Probably at home it would but not here,' said Gwynneth, 'I wonder how Belstead got you a pass? Oh well, bugger Belstead. That's his look out. I expect he thought that without a contract you wouldn't know about those standard clauses agreeing to keep his hands off your arse. I've got one of my contracts here. Sign it now. Have you got your passport with you?' Catrina tapped her bag. 'Then let's just go over to the pass office immediately and see what we can pull off.'

Half an hour later Catrina emerged with a fresh set of documents, a new pass and a spring in her step.

There had, of course, been obstacles. It was impossible, the Parliamentary official had stated bluntly. Such a matter would take at least two weeks. They had had no notification. There was something, though, in the way Madame Price had peered through him, smiled, then peered through him again without saying a word that had brought a mumbled 'maybe in this case...' and a little flurry of forms.

In Roger Belstead's office Nigel and Peregrine were playing a computer game and on the phone to a girl friend respectively. They failed to notice as Catrina switched off her own terminal, gathered a bagful of personal bits and papers, and her coat.

'Just popping out,' she announced breezily.

Too late Nigel called after her. 'When will you be back?'

~~~

An Offer Or Not

Catrina was not the only one of the habitués of Café Franck to have new job prospects that Wednesday morning. The conversations Mercedes had had with the dapper little Italian the night before had borne fruit, or at least the blossom was looking promising. She had not really settled down to anything special since arriving in Brussels that summer.

After finishing her MA in economics and European studies in Valencia, her assumption had been that there was unlikely to be any decent work to be had in Spain, where so few of her friends were finding it that the cafés were becoming more gathering places for the despondent unemployed than burgeoning intellectuals. Brussels had seemed a clever idea. She could escape the worst of the southern summer heat, which she loathed, Brussels was not especially expensive, and she had saved just about enough to rent a small place while she studied to take the European Commission's entrance exams.

In theory this was still what she was doing. As the summer had turned to autumn, however, and she had found reasons and excuses to peek inside the European Commission's buildings, the less enamoured she had become.

For a start, it didn't seem to matter which Directorate-General you were in, the offices, with their grey doors, seemed to be the same size and the same dispiriting uniformity. Not only was it impossible to distinguish what actually happened in any of them, the pasty faces of her potential colleagues, and the piles of cigarette ends outside the entrances, were hardly an advert for an exciting career. Mercedes thought of all the demoralised bureaucrats she had seen at home and came to realise fast that the security of public service came at a cost. Even in the international and altruistic world of Europe's custodians, it was too easy to become just another plodding functionary.

At twenty-seven Mercedes still had her ideals. She was not entirely sure what they were but she was certain that they did not include boring herself to death – or at least until motherhood gave her something else to think about.

The dapper Italian had given her an alternative. A new public relations company was opening, specialising in helping Mediterranean organisations and companies with their lobbying. They had decided that they wanted to recruit only in Brussels, and only by personal contacts, direct or indirect. A friend of a friend had recommended Mercedes. Hence the assignation in Café Franck the night before.

At half past ten on Wednesday morning Mercedes had come back into the café, ordered her latte from Patrice and deliberately returned to the same table to consider her position. Patrice, recognising her from the debacle of Saturday, had been extra attentive. Without her, he thought but didn't say as the coffee dripped through it's filter and he frothed the milk, he would never have met Catrina.

The first thing Mercedes had to consider was whether Paolo, for that was his name, had really offered her a job or just talked about it a lot. He had spoken in Italian at the start of their meeting, assuming that the Valencian girl would understand but, when it became clear she was struggling with his more nuanced points, had switched to English. In this, Mercedes could understand better but Paolo – by nature a speaker with a florid turn of phrase in any language, was even less clear. He had talked about the company he represented, Umberto Carraldo e Filio, outlined the ambitious plans, told her where the offices were and outlined the work he needed to be done.

But had he actually offered her the job? She realised with a grimace that she had completely failed to ask and, even more stupidly, forgotten to leave with any idea of how much he was offering to pay. Maybe she was just a green ex-student with no idea of the real world, as José and her father never tired of telling her.

Pondering, Mercedes gathered her bag, left her scarf draped across her seat to save it, and went to the counter. She nodded when Patrice offered to make her another Latte and paid for a croissant from the pile in a basket too.

'You are OK today?' Patrice asked as he gave her her change.

Mercedes smiled absently, 'Yes, thank you.'

'No accidents then, I hope?' solicited Patrice but by then Mercedes was already wandering back to her table. Patrice shrugged and turned to his next customer. If she did not want to make conversation that was her business.

There was only one way to find out, of course. After Mercedes had eaten the croissant and drunk half the coffee she reached into her handbag and pulled out Paulo's card and her phone. Automatically before dialling she checked for texts and emails. There were three inconsequential ones from Spain and a couple from her companions, the boys who had been such dead losses over the weekend. She scrolled down. Fifth on the list in the emails she spotted Paulo's name and clicked on the message.

'Cara,' it began but then belied the endearment. 'I much enjoyed our meeting yesterday evening and I am sure that one day we could work together with profit. But, misericordia!, I fear it will not be immediately. I am instructed to employ a young lady from our office in Torino and I cannot refuse. Perhaps in the Spring?'

Mercedes clicked off the phone and gulped some coffee.

Tears began to well. Don't be silly, she tried to tell herself, he was never serious and anyway, you didn't want that job.

Yes she did, she admitted as she walked across the square, dodged the busses and began to climb the hill towards Avenue Louise.

Half way up she paused out of habit and looked in at the window of Nikita's gallery. The Russian woman, phone to her ear, spotted Mercedes and waved, signalling her to come in.

In the gallery she stood, peering, without seeing, at a particularly gruesome nude slapped in red onto a puce background and waited for Nikita to finish her call. Eventually it happened and Nikita strolled over.

'My dear, how lovely. How are you this morning?'

The question could hardly have been more innocent or conventional but Mercedes made the mistake of thinking about it and, after the lip had quivered for a second, burst into tears.

'Whatever is wrong?' asked Nikita, putting an arm around her shoulders and guiding her towards the back of the gallery. Mercedes told her.

The Russian's reaction was the last thing the Valencian had expected. 'Oh, don't worry about that. I'm so glad. I've been thinking about this since yesterday and I was going to call you after lunch. Why don't you come and work for me?'

~~~

A Difference Of Viewpoint

Fidel was plotting – at least he liked to think he was. In reality he was sitting in his favourite corner of Café Franck smiling a little distractedly as Elise and Kathrin discussed his future across the table, seemingly as though whether he was there or not could hardly have been less relevant.

The particular future they had in mind, apparently, involved him being the public face but not the academic driving force, of the Utterly Free University (UFU) that was beginning to take paper shape. Kathrin had the outline of a business plan, Elise had the makings of a prospectus. Both were bold, original and, in Fidel's view, utterly baffling. It seemed he would no longer need to go to his old office, redecorated or not.

Serried ranks of students, or the empty seats in which they were meant to have listened to him from, would no longer gaze at him in admiration or stupefaction. Indeed he need never leave his flat. All his lectures would be 'live streamed and podcast' as he sat in his armchair (shelves of books as the backdrop). Students would dial him up, day or night (Elise joked, though Fidel found it thoroughly unfunny) for a video tutorial. In fact, she pointed out, in the UFU he would never actually meet his students in the flesh and she said it as if denying him the 'flesh' was the main purpose of the exercise. Fidel wondered how this sliver of a girl had taken such firm and exclusive control of his life only five days since he had first invited her across his threshold.

Did he like it? He drank her with his eyes and decided nothing could make him happier.

He began to listen with a little more concentration and the pleasure dissipated. There would be online forums, Elise was expounding to Kathrin, interactive debates, virtual encounters and something disturbingly called a transparent permanent record and recall examination and essay submission system (TPRREESS or TRESPASS). Fidel thought about his higgledy-piggledy piles of scripts and essays, each with its indecipherable scrawl of tart criticism. He knew no other way to mark.

So what? Kathrin curled her lip slightly as she countered him. If he wanted to be Neanderthal he could print the damn things out, scribble on them to his heart's content, and upload his comments afterwards. But it would triple the time it took him to deal with them. Fidel sipped his coffee morosely. He was going off the whole idea fast.

Furthermore, he was informed, the student community would be global. No physical proximity or even national residency was necessary. Students could be in Mongolia or Antarctica, it mattered not. That meant he would have to teach in English, of course, Kathrin remarked as though it was so obvious there could be no debate.

Now Fidel was thoroughly alarmed. His French was the main weapon of his intellect. In French he constructed theories and arguments that were as elegant as they were inconclusive. In Flemish too he could just about fulminate with authority. But English! It was a language for mechanics and bankers. No serious social thinker could express his discipline in English. It was like asking a Japanese silk painter to use industrial acrylic.

As the two young women warmed to their themes, Fidel started to rumble. Had they known him for a little longer they would have realised that this was not a good sign. The rumble was volcanic. It started quietly, a vague vibration deep in the throat that was sensed rather than heard. It bubbled and as it bubbled Fidel started to rock slowly. A rhythm emerged as the rumble moved up a tone or two. It began to have the makings of song, if a song laden with threat.

What would be really great, Kathrin suggested, would be if students could send their work in any language and an instant translation tool would convert them into something Fidel could understand. Conversely his contributions could be translated in subtitle form in real time. Yes, there would be inaccuracies and occasional misunderstandings but think of the speed, the innovation, the open access!

The rumble became a groan, almost a bass keening.

Elise was reaching a peak of enthusiasm. There could be an app, she cried. On any student's clever phone an icon could be tapped which would bring Fidel to them live, or at least upload his latest tutorial and even the whole archive for the course.

Then, wherever they were, the student could just text him a reply, a comment, a correction and he would be by their virtual side in seconds.

The rumble reached the caldera of Fidel's volcano. 'I am not...,' he began but for a moment was shaking too much to continue. He clenched his fist and slammed it into the table top. 'I am not...,' he rose to his feet.

'Not what?' enquired Kathrin, unimpressed.

'I am not,' he was shouting now, 'a toy. I am not a plaything for students. No, no, no and again no!'

Elise and Kathrin gazed at him in astonishment.

'But, love, why not?' Elise asked in genuine surprise.

'No, and that is final.' Fidel announced, gathered his hat and strode out of the building.

The girls watched him go, looked at each and grimaced. Elise was too hurt to say 'silly old fool' but Kathrin had no qualms. 'Who cares?' she said. 'We don't need him anyway. There are plenty of teachers who will embrace this, who will understand the possibilities, who have ambition.'

But she had misjudged her audience once again. Elise could feel the tears beginning to well up as she watched Fidel hunch his coat about his shoulders and walk furiously across the square.

'I must go.' Elise knew that this was a real crisis, a moment when life could go either way. Stay and she could develop an idea but lose everything that had taken shape over the last week. She abandoned the table and ran after him.

~~~

Considerations

After Mercedes had left, but before the main morning coffee brigade subtly morphed into the lunchtime throng, Patrice had a break long enough to make a grand café for himself and amble outside for a smoke. It was a moment to stop and consider.

None of his regulars were in the café at that moment, except for Kathrin and he was not really on conversational terms with her. To be honest, she scared him a little. He nodded to her as she left while he was lighting his cigarette. Across the square he caught a glimpse of Elise catching up with Fidel and taking his arm to cross the street between the trams.

Now there was a strange liaison.

Fidel had been a fixture in the Café Franck ever since Patrice had been working there and, he suspected, a quarter of a century before that. Had he known his building history, Patrice would have noticed that his dates didn't quite add up. The café had not been open that long. It was true, though, that Fidel had been one of those campaigning and petitioning for the splendid 1930s edifice of Flagey to be saved from developers when RTBF, the Belgian French broadcaster, had abandoned it in the 1990s.

The café, despite it's air of permanence, was newer than Fidel's presence in Flagey. Thirty years earlier, sometime around 1983, would have found him and his young iconoclasts in the smoking bar across the road and, in truth, the patron of the Le Pitch-pin had never quite forgiven him for his desertion to the trendy competitor when it opened later.

Fidel had had a better reason than mere change of scene, though: something that both Patrice and Elise had yet to discover. In those far off days, when Fidel had been in his late thirties, he had campaigned for the retention of the building and the orchestra resident in it, not because of architectural or musical passion, but because he was in love with one of the viola players in the orchestra – and her name was also Elise. She might not have been learning Modern Circus Studies but, Fidel would have recalled, his old Elise did things on a water bed that were well worth a dissertation or two.

Patrice was thinking along different but similar lines as his cigarette reached the halfway point. The young Elise had never really crossed his consciousness except behind the bar but now her friendship with Fidel caused him to consider her. He had brushed against her once or twice as they shimmied past each other to and from the coffee machine but, since she had no figure to speak of, had given her little more than a cursory glance – the glance all heterosexual men give all girls as they move around them. Watching her as she began to climb the hill in the distance with Fidel, he decided he was not missing much.

His thoughts turned to Catrina instead and immediately

became complicated. He smiled. It had been a weekend full of novelty. She was English, for a start. He had never had an English lover and had always believed that such a thing was among the least desirable options a boy could have. All those games, the social expectations and distinctions, the lack of finesse or passion, the nervousness.

He had to admit, though, that most of his preconceptions had been thrown out of the window of Catrina's tiny apartment somewhere around the half hour mark. Except the nervousness, and that he had, to his surprise, found rather charming. It was a relief not to have a lover who, like the French girls, knew everything about love-making and marked him out of ten while he put his clothes on.

Catrina clearly adored him, or at least seemed to. One could never really tell. The question was whether he felt the same way. So far he was not sure. She was delightful but... He left the thought hanging.

Patrice glanced back into the café. There was no queue at the bar. His colleague was coping fine. There was time for another cigarette. He lit one and gazed across the lake, withdrawing a little under the overhang of the building as spots of rain began to drift down.

He was not given to introspection, especially when it came to analysing his lovers. It was one of the great joys of working behind a bar that you were meeting new women all the time. Usually any flirtation went no further than a smile across the mint tea and a brief touch as the money changed hands, as they had in his first remembered contact with Catrina. But rather more than occasionally things continued, harmlessly enough most of the time. Enough ladies had let him follow them to bed to make any other form of work lose its attraction, even if the money was better.

Patrice was 28, though, and his parents were beginning to get on his back about getting a 'real' job, whatever that was meant to be. He thought of the lives his customers led, or that he imagined they led. Would he happier? Too hard to know.

He had heard enough frustrations in the pillow talk to realise that nothing was ever perfect. But then his mind went back to the start of the day; how he had had to be home early the night before in order to be up in time for the morning shift. No Catrina to wake up with, not much of interest in the day, and a pleasant drift through the evening. Could be better, could be worse.

Patrice finished his second cigarette and stubbed it into the tin bin at his elbow. Back to the grind. The rain was becoming more determined. He became aware of words being shouted from an outside table, placed next to the window a few metres along, just out of reach of the water.

'Hey you!'

Patrice could have sworn he heard the old French command of 'garçon' – hardly likely to endear the demander to the new generation of bar staff. Café Franck did not have waiters. People were expected to come to the bar in the British manner. Patrice looked over.

'About time. We need some service here,' a middle-aged man in a suit barked back.

That decided it – and the direction of Patrice's meditation on his life. He raised his middle finger in salute, turned, and went back to his post. Things would have to change.

~~~

The Fates Dance

As Patrice returned to duty behind the bar his first customer was Flamand, asking for a drop of caramel sirop in his milky coffee and a glass of iced water to accompany it. Patrice obliged but struggled to hide his disdain at the ingénue tastes of the soft young man in front of him. Flamand, though, noticed nothing, paid, and carried his collection of liquids back to a window table close to the radiator.

From his calico bag, slung over the back of the chair, Flamand extracted a slender ipad and his new moleskin notebook. It was a toss-up which, screen or paper, he was going to use. On the one hand there was this serious essay on Maupassant due in on the following Monday morning. On the other, there was equally serious writing to be done in praise of Agnestina. She was the love of his life, he was sure. Agnestina thought he might be a happy diversion until Christmas but he was not to know that.

Flamand's finger flicked impatiently across the surface of the ipad, occasionally tapping on the screen if something caught half his attention. Now and then a reference caught his eye and he book-marked it. He pulled up the beginnings of his own essay, which he had emailed himself earlier, and added a couple of sentences. Even he realised they contained no great insights into the depths of French literature. He took a sip of his sticky coffee, washed it off his lips with the water, and sighed.

The wind blew the curtains surrounding the door, announcing a new arrival. Flamand glanced up instinctively, or perhaps just in hope that the breeze was blowing Agnestina his way.

It didn't. Instead the Wagnerian figure of Louise wafted in and sailed majestically towards the bar. There she saw and recognised Patrice. He was the last person she had wanted to see and it had taken all her nerve to walk into Café Franck after the painful events of the weekend.

There was a moment of tension, a pause as she remembered his protection of Catrina while she, Louise, had lain stricken on the cold paving. Then Patrice's professionalism triumphed and Louise smiled as she also remembered the outcome of their encounter. She was not to know it had also been the catalyst for Patrice's own affair.

'Madame?' Patrice enquired.

Louise nearly spoiled Patrice's mood again by ordering a mint tea but then switched and asked for a red wine. She really shouldn't, this was a clandestine visit to the café on the way back to her office after a meeting of stupefying dullness but, what the heck, if one was skiving one might as well skive properly. Everything was in the wrong order. She had avoided Le Pitch-pin because it's mint tea was not have as good as the Café Franck's and here she was ordering wine in the latter where it was much worse.

Patrice inclined his head and reached for glass and bottle. 'I hope, he asked as he poured, 'Madame has recovered from the nasty fall?'

'Nearly,' admitted Louise, 'just a bruise left and my knee is a little sore but otherwise...'

'I'm glad to hear it,' said Patrice as Louise searched in her purse for coins. 'No, Madame, this glass is on me: perhaps a little consolation?'

Louise looked up in amazement and smiled enormously. It was the last gesture she had expected. 'That's so kind,' she said, and meant it.

'Not at all.'

She took a first drink to stop wine spilling, carried the rest over to a spare table by the window and began to settle herself. Looking up, she caught the frown on the face of the willowy youth gazing at her from the next table and wished she could have lent him some of the good humour that had spread over her with Patrice's gift.

The frown that Flamand was sporting was in fact caused entirely by Louise, or at least by the fact and scale of Louise. If she sat there he could not see the doorway properly. And if he couldn't see the door, he would not be able to spot Agnestina if she did arrive. He was not expecting her, it was true, but she knew he was in Café Franck (he had sent her a text saying so) and she might, just might, decide to join him.

Louise had another taste of her wine and turned her attention, through the window, across the lake to the building that housed her own flat. The scrum of TV crews that had littered the pavement of the next block the day before had dispersed and the scene had returned to its usual tranquillity, lit by a pale autumn sun between the showers. A flight of ducks touched down on the water, squabbled, dipped and took to the sky for another circuit or two. A man and a woman, coming from opposite directions, allowed their dogs to greet each other, followed the example, then passed on along the lakeside. A few seconds later the gentle scene was broken by a pair of number 71 buses, between their articulated sections long enough to fill the whole of the street view. Louise grunted and returned to her wine.

The skinny young man at the opposing table, she noticed, had changed tables and now sat so that he could see round her, poring over a notebook with his head resting on his left hand. Dreaming or thinking, Louise wondered?

The answer, Flamand could have told her, was neither. He was composing. He had given up on old French literature and was trying his best to create some of his own, working on a villanelle in honour of Agnestina.

Louise glanced at her watch. She really must appear back in the office before lunchtime, otherwise her colleagues would realise she had done more than simply return from the tedious meeting. She drained the last of her wine, stood, dressed to leave, and carried her empty glass back to the bar. Patrice watched as she arrived in front of him.

'Another,' he suggested.

'No, no. Not so early,' smiled Louise, 'but thank you.'

'No problem,' said Patrice, and it was true. Louise might be a long way from his ideal woman but she was charming and had graciousness that he could appreciate, especially given the manners of most of the customers.

He watched as, at the exit, the door was held open by a girl with subtle red-blonde hair of simply ravishing beauty. Louise thanked her and started to leave but then paused to check for her office pass. The girl came halfway to the bar and looked round the café. It was Flamand's bad fortune that at just that moment he dropped his pen and bent to retrieve it.

And so Agnestina looked down at her mobile phone, gave a little grimace, turned on her heel and disappeared the way she had come. Had she not, the villanelle might never have been completed but Flamand's day would have been far happier.

~~~

Return Coup

If Esko and Amelie had thought that a day would be enough to calm the press they were soon disabused. In Esko's office Mariana was no longer fielding calls as much as hurling their startled makers hard against a virtual wall. Had they made the mistake of appearing in person, they would have risked defenestration from the 10th floor of Parliamentary tower block G. More than one smirking parliamentarian did try to cross the office threshold but was clever enough to realise the risk involved from the sheer intensity of the glare that Mariana had summoned up from the depths of her Karelian ancestry. Just try it, the glare said, and discover the true meaning of arctic wastes.

Esko himself was not so bothered, regarding the whole fuss with amused if slightly bored tolerance. His statement of no comment, other than that his wife and he had separated, had deflected attention back to Finland and, in Brussels, to Amelie's agent. To the Belgian and French press he was just an unknown foreign politician and a man.

Amelie, though, was a very different kettle of fish (or, since this was Brussels, moules). She was young, beautiful, French, a film starlet and, above all, in town trying to promote a film.

Amelie was followed and photographed, surrounded and hounded until she decided it was impossible to leave her hotel room in the Conrad.

That proved not to be too much of an inconvenience. The hotel was used to being the retreat of ministers attending summits and its security staff were only too happy to provide the sort of visible discouragement necessary. Reporters were politely but forcefully put in their place, which was either a corral in the furthest corner of the lobby, or the least fashionable of the hotel's bars – and they were only allowed there as long as they promised not to interfere with guests. They spent much of the day talking to each other and inventing non-existent titbits to keep the story alive and their impressive bar bills paid.

Amelie herself was unperturbed. Cheered by all the press attention, none of it generated by themselves, her film company had moved her into a full suite (previous occupant, the Slovak Prime Minister) and installed a junior press officer to deal with all the calls. Amelie switched mobiles and texted only Esko and her mother the number. Twitter was left to the press officers, who duly tweeted utter balderdash on her behalf, all of which was designed to boost the new film's notoriety.

The whole thing would kick off soon enough, since she was due at four o'clock on Brussels' favourite early evening chat show.

The Finnish press had never heard of Amelie and, anyway, Esko was only an MEP, so the full entertainment was unlikely to break until the weekend when the domestic reporters could file the results of their stalking of Rikka, Esko's wife, who was Helsinki based. She might have been able to have sold the story of the wronged spouse quite highly if she had not, on that Wednesday, been spotted lunching a little more fondly than was quite businesslike with one of the rising baritones at the Helsinki Opera House.

Back on the 10th floor of European Parliament Block G, Mariana was in full crisis by the middle of the afternoon. While the principal characters in the drama of unfolding affairs were relaxing into their new notoriety without too much bother, Mariana was aware that events were leaving her long cherished role as Esko's lover in waiting far, far behind. The problem was that it was a role only cherished by her. Esko himself was not only oblivious but enough of a northern European correct political not to entertain the idea of bedding his researcher. Had he been Italian it would have been another matter. But he was not and would not. Mariana didn't see why not, however.

Her fellow assistant, a dull boy of twenty-four from (as far as Mariana was concerned) Tampere, had called in sick all week and so was missing all the drama. There was no-one in the office for Mariana even to be horrible to.

The main voting in the Parliament was over for the week and that meant Esko was free to lunch with a group of lobbyists, and hold meetings with representatives of two worthy human rights organisations, before heading back to his offices for about five minutes until a committee reconvened at three.

He charged in by the private door, chucked the accumulated brochures, position papers and other collected detritus onto the desk and looked for his committee papers, which Mariana usually placed assiduously in the middle of the desk. There were none.

Her boss frowned, checked his computer screen, ignored the emails, then went over to open the connecting door to the assistants' office.

Mariana was standing immediately in front of it on the other side, waiting for just this moment. Instead of greeting him with a handful of papers, Mariana was holding nothing. It was time, she had decided after sobbing for most of the previous three hours, to take matters into her own hands. She had therefore spent the best part of lunchtime in the ladies toilet working on her make-up.

She had the fight of her life on her hands if she was to make Esko realise there was more to love than film stars. Subtlety was not the tactic for now.

So when the door opened and Esko walked through she was ready for him. The outer door to her office was locked, the window blinds were drawn down. More importantly her long brown hair was shaken loose, her shirt hung outside her trousers and was open, fully open with nothing else to obstruct the view.

Esko glanced and gulped but before he could either protest or retreat, Mariana's arms were round his neck and her lips were reaching for his. Esko did the only thing he thought was fair in the circumstances. Nothing. He kept his mouth shut and arms to his sides.

Eventually, against the cliff that Esko had become, Mariana's assault collapsed and the frenzy was instead replaced with tears. Esko buttoned her shirt, gave her a hug, said, 'bring the papers to the Committee room. We'll talk about this later,' and retreated back into his office.

Much later, he decided, as he in turn locked the doors and made his way to the lifts.

~~~

New Jobs

Catrina alighted from the 38 bus on Flagey and made her way across the open square towards the Café Franck just as the sun was setting that autumn Wednesday evening. Her mood was inclined to the skittish and she walked without the heavy tread and distracted air that she only now realised had dogged her for months, ever since the euphoria of moving out of Derby into the exotic (by Derby standards) world of Brussels had started to fade. The realities of life (the revolting boss, Belstead MEP, and intolerable sort-of boyfriend, Bruno) had weighed her down.

In under a week all that had changed. She was not a woman to walk on air. There was a slight lack of co-ordination about her movements that suggested that, had she tried to walk on air, she would have fallen off.

Nonetheless, when Patrice saw her push her way through the curtain into the café he hardly recognised her for a moment. She looked younger, better dressed, flowing. He let the beer run over his hand as he poured and it took a nudge in the back from his fellow barman before he remembered to flip off the tap. His misgivings of a few hours earlier fell away.

Catrina spotted him looking at her and grinned as she sauntered across the room.

'Hello,' she said. There was a pause while Patrice leaned over the bar to kiss her. He was still holding the glass of beer, which tipped, of course, and half emptied onto the floor. Patrice shrugged like a clown and started the pouring again.

Next to Catrina the intended recipient of the beer, one of the few men wearing a tie in Café Franck, glared and began to tap a two euro piece on the chrome bar. It was not a clever move. In an instant Patrice poured away the rest of the drink, moved three paces to his right and took another order. The tie wearer would wait all night and still not be served again.

'Hello,' a voice said. It was not Catrina this time, though, but Mercedes. Yet there was a jauntiness in the greeting that was not far off the tone that Catrina herself had used half a minute earlier. Patrice's good humour returned as he looked out at the two women. Would they remember each other from their first disastrous encounter a few days before, he wondered?

'Oh, hello,' said Catrina, glancing across and down, instantly embarrassed by the memories of spilt mint tea, Mercedes' scalded back, and all the confusion and acrimony that had followed. She instantly deflated, her devil-may-care air banished as a momentary lapse.

Mercedes, on the other hand, was still bubbling. 'I'm so happy,' she began to Patrice.

He reached out and held Catrina's shoulder. 'Hear that? So don't look sad again.' He turned back to the Spanish girl, 'and why so happy?'

'I have a new job,' she exclaimed and, beaming, turned to Catrina, 'and I didn't realise until I was offered it, I wanted a job like it so much.'

It was Catrina's turn for the zest to spray, 'But so have I!' To Patrice, 'that's what I came to tell you.'

'Superb,' said Patrice, 'then we must celebrate.' He looked along the bar and at his colleagues. 'I cannot leave just now,' he admitted, 'it is getting busy but,' he indicated the seats at the bar further round the L shape, the ones where the bearded man had sat when Elise had slipped ice down his shirt while he was necking the evening before, 'sit there and I can bring something.'

The two women nodded and shifted themselves. Along the way Catrina's British habits forced their way to the front. As they gathered their bags, she said, 'I'm Catrina, by the way, and I'm still so sorry for last Saturday.'

The Spaniard just said, 'Mercedes, that's OK,' but for

Catrina it was enough. Her cultural domestic gods were propitiated.

They settled themselves down at the bar and there was a new companionable silence while they waited for Patrice to return with their drinks. They hadn't actually ordered any but both were getting used to Patrice's habit of deciding that they wanted what he wanted them to have. They were rarely disappointed. This time he appeared with three cocktails topped with mint leaves and lime in hand. Catrina raised an eyebrow.

'We all remember the little accident with mint tea...'

'Naturally,' said Catrina with a grimace.

'But it was a good accident,' Patrice persisted, 'it brought us all together. Without it...? So in its honour I have Mojitos. They will not burn but they will refresh. Santé.'

They all clinked glasses and sipped through straws.

'Now tell me,' resumed Patrice, 'these new jobs?'

Catrina naturally deferred to Mercedes. Mercedes, equally naturally, was not in the habit of deferring. 'I have been looking,' she began, 'but I had no idea for what. I thought of the Parliament...'

'Don't!' said Catrina with feeling.

'... but that did not feel right. I thought of going home but, you know, there are no jobs in Spain if you are our age and do not have connections, and then last night I met this Italian man who talked about lobbying and public relations.'

'You got it, well done,' Catrina said.

'No, he turned me down. This morning I was desperate. I was walking up to Avenue Louise and, you know that gallery, Nikita's?'

'Yes.'

'She asked me in. I'm afraid I cried.'

Patrice sipped his drink and decided it was safer not to comment. Catrina just said, 'I'm not surprised,' and her look at Patrice dared him to crack any remark back.

'She's so kind,' Mercedes went on. 'She has asked me to work for her in the gallery, part time at first. But it is enough. I love it already.'

'Fantastic,' enthused Patrice as much as he could before looking to Catrina, 'and you? You have left the Parliament?'

She shook her head. 'No, just bloody Belstead. I've swapped the far right for the far-ish left. Still British, of course, but Plaid Cymru.'

Patrice looked baffled.

'The Party of Wales,' Catrina explained with her new-found Celtic pride. The Belgian and the Spaniard still looked baffled.

'Galles, Pays de Galles', she tried again.

'Oh, I see,' said Mercedes, her interest evaporating.

For Catrina a new experience was surfacing: that of adopted protective possessiveness. It was the first time this middle English girl had ever had the slightest sympathy with the West of her big island. But if being constantly dismissed as irrelevant was what that country's adherents had to put up with, then she was on their side. After all, being dismissed as irrelevant was what men (apart from Patrice she had to admit) had been doing to her for years.

~~~

Cocktail Hour

Catrina, Mercedes and Patrice were halfway down their second Mojitos when Elise pushed through the curtains into Café Franck. She hovered. She had wanted to talk to Patrice but she had also wanted to sit on the stool where Catrina was sitting and have a serious talk. Now not only was Catrina in place but there was a jollity to the atmosphere that ill matched her own need to deal with turmoil. She thought about turning on her heel and leaving, perhaps going for a morose drink on her own under the leering eyes of the old men playing cards across the tram lines at Le Pitch-pin.

The thought came too late. Patrice spotted her and waved her over to the spare stool next to Catrina. Elise smiled wanly, inclined her head and took up the offer. Patrice was already into the ritual of preparing her a Mojito to match those remaining on the bar.

'Hi,' said Catrina with the cheerfulness of one who has already had a cocktail and is generally enchanted with the world.

'Hi,' returned Elise without the same enthusiasm and stared intently at the chrome of the bar as she waited for Patrice to return.

Her lack of zip deflated Catrina a touch too. She in turn began to stare at the green contents of her glass as if they held a whole dictionary of answers. Earlier in the day she would have jumped in with an encouraging 'what's up?' but she was all too aware that her recent record with that phrase was not a good one. She had not minded in the slightest when Mariana and Bruno had huffed away from her table at lunchtime in the Parliament the day before but she did not really want to have the same effect on Elise. She liked her too much, for one thing, but more importantly, though she was mildly disgusted with herself for having to admit it, she did not want Elise throwing herself into Patrice's arms for comfort, whatever the quality of the solace he could provide. If Elise was in a state of emotional stress, then Catrina wanted her firmly on her side of the bar, not Patrice's.

They glanced at each other a couple of times, managed a smile, then went back to their contemplation of the space in front. Catrina turned to Mercedes but she seemed to have been numbed out of conversation by Elise's mood too.

After a minute or two, in which he had been distracted from Elise's cocktail by some desperate calls for two beers and a bottle of rosé, Patrice returned and triumphantly presented her with his creation.

'Salut', he said with the same zest with which Catrina had said 'hi'.

Elise said nothing but took a strawful of alcohol. Across the bar Patrice caught Catrina's glance and raised an eyebrow. She gave a miniscule shrug and lowered one corner of her mouth.

With the practised art of the professional barman as mood changer, Patrice lifted his own glass. 'We have to celebrate, cherie. Catrina has a new job. She has left the pay of the British right for the left of Pays de Galles!'

'Oh.' It was neither an interested question nor an exclamation of surprise. Just a flat note in monochrome voice.

'And she has told her ex-boyfriend to get totally lost.'

'Oh.'

'So she is very happy. I am very happy.'

'Ah, that's good'.

'Yes, and this is Mercedes – ah, you know. She has a new job and she is happy too.' Patrice gave up and took a tug at his drink, then slipped away to attend to his duties.

Elise drank until at least half the contents of the glass were gone and she was matching Catrina's.

'You look as though you could do with another one of those,' suggested Catrina.

'You may be right. But not a cocktail this time, I think. Maybe Bailey's.' She finished off the mint then, with a visible effort, turned to Catrina and changed her tone of voice. 'So, you had a good day – a break. Congratulations.'

'Thanks. It seems the same was not true for you, though.'

'Maybe, maybe not. I don't know yet. It seems that way but...' Elise lapsed back into silence.

Patrice broke away long enough for them both to order and Catrina decided to change the subject. In fact she was taking the plunge when she asked, 'And how is your idea for Fidel and Hugo's new university going?'

It was instantly clear this was most, if not all, the problem.

'It is not. There will be no UFU. At least, not with Fidel and therefore not with me.'

'Oh?' Catrina managed, unlike Elise, to convey surprise, disappointment, sympathy and inquiry in the syllable.

'He does not want it. He is afraid. It is too new – no, it is just new. He is so...'

'Timid?' suggested Catrina.

'Chicken,' announced Elise with disgust.

'What chicken?' asked Patrice as he placed fresh and full glasses in front of them.

'The chicken Fidel,' Elise almost spat.

'He's not going to go along with Elise's idea for the online university. It's too risky for him,' explained the English girl.

'You mean he is comfortable as he is. Well,' observed Patrice, 'I'm not surprised. He is famous in this square of Flagey and on cable TV, and he is not so young. Maybe it is enough.'

Elise downed her Bailey's in one gulp and pushed the empty glass forward for a refill. 'Then enough will not include me,' she announced with decision.

'Are you sure?' asked Catrina with all the insecurity of one in love who would forego any brilliant career move rather than renounce her lover, and looked at Patrice adoringly as he reached behind him for the bottle of creamed whiskey.

'Naturally I am sure.'

To their right the curtains billowed as the door of Café Franck was opened to the evening breeze. Fidel shambled in. He paused, gazed across to where Elise, Mercedes and Catrina sat, looking as crestfallen as his erstwhile companion.

Haltingly he made his way over and stood between them. Elise did not bother to turn but Catrina put a welcoming hand on his arm.

'Elise,' he started, 'I am a fool, such a fool. It's a wonderful idea. Of course it is. If it is your idea it must be. I can live with or without a university but I cannot do without you. Not just now.'

'You mean it?'

Fidel nodded, 'I mean it', and caught Elise as she fell off the stool trying to clasp him in her arms.

VI

Thursday

A Satisfactory Committee

Thursday morning in the European Parliament could be a strange time in Committee Week. The committees were in full session but most of the MEPs themselves had every intention of leaving at lunchtime, either for domestic engagements in their own countries or to speak at one of the endless European conferences on their pet subjects that would lead into the weekend. These were likely to be in the most far-flung cities of the Union, held in the parts Brussels' politics rarely reached, just to make them feel wanted.

Either way, after the mics were turned off, a rush to the airport and a baguette along the way was likely to be most members' routine for the afternoon. This being the case, many of them sent their assistants to mind the committee and waited in their offices for a text to summon them if anything interesting looked like happening - or an agenda item was reached on which they particularly wanted to speak.

For Esko that Thursday, the arrangement solved what would otherwise have been an embarrassing problem.

His assistant, Mariana, was still in emotional shock after declaring her infatuation with such abandon the previous morning. She had no clue as to how she should deal with their first encounter in the office since. Should she sit meekly behind her desk and pretend it had never happened? That would be the Finnish way. Or should she tender her resignation as soon as Esko walked in? There didn't seem to be too many options in between.

The committee meeting saved them from both eventualities, or at least postponed them. Mariana gathered some papers and found the room, in an obscure backwater of the Leo building in which the Parliament's Civil Liberties and Justice (not always the same thing) Committee was sitting, before Esko appeared. He himself made sure that he was late and so, with a relieved sigh, found a nicely deserted office.

He spent a quiet hour looking through emails and CVs from prospective interns before a text from Mariana announced that a vote was about to be taken on a report into the comparative behaviour of police forces in demonstrations. It was, he knew, a subject on which Mariana had very decided views. The report, drafted by a Bulgarian of the old school, suggested that far firmer action should be taken on all occasions, with crowds being broken up and detained at the first opportunity. Esko knew that he would not just please Mariana by voting against it; there would be a solid majority opposed on the left and centre of the committee, and, he suspected, from most moderates on the right as well.

The seating arrangements in the semicircle of the meeting rooms meant that Mariana was in the middle three rows from the back while Esko had his assigned place at the same position four rows in front of her. There did not have to be an immediate encounter.

Mariana watched him steadily as he shuffled round the backs of his fellow members, grabbing a shoulder or two in friendly greeting along the way. As he reached his seat he turned, caught her eye and smiled warmly. Mariana gave a curt nod and looked down at her papers but it was no good – she realised the blood was rushing to her head hopelessly.

To her relief, by the time she looked up again Esko had sat down with his back to her and was in earnest conversation with the Lithuanian member next to him.

The voting on the report started, points of order were taken, the stream of clause and paragraph numbers flowed by until the Bulgarian rapporteur stormed out, resoundingly defeated and supported by few except the Hungarian, Greek and Spanish ultra nationalists. Since most of the right wing parties of Europe were themselves as heavily into holding demonstrations on their capitals' streets as those on the left, the rapporteur's demand that police should be a bit more brutal was always going to be a loser.

The session closed, the other members stayed for a few

moments, sharing wry asides at his discomfort, then began to drift away.

A few of the NGO observers, freed from the etiquette of having to stay in the back rows during the debate, wandered down to thank or berate their contacts among the members. One made his way over to Esko and waited patiently at his shoulder until the Finn had finished his conversation with the bespectacled and tousled-haired Lithuanian – a philosopher by profession until his country had realised it was short of MEP material and he had compared the salary with that which he had as a part-time member of the faculty at the University of Vilnius.

As the flow of intellectual observation flowed on, Esko looked up at the tall blond man waiting patiently and smiled encouragement before turning back to his loquacious companion.

'That's great, Vytautas,' Esko interrupted, 'maybe we can carry this on later – perhaps over a beer some time?'

The philosopher finished his paragraph-long sentence undeterred, grinned disarmingly, and ambled off.

The blond man took his chance. 'I'm sorry if I interrupted,' he began.

'I'm very relieved you did,' sighed Esko. 'We could have

missed the rest of today otherwise.'

'Thank you. I am Dirk van Abcoude. I am with European Writers Against Injustice – EWAI.'

'Are there any in favour of it?' asked Esko mischievously.

'I'm sorry?'

'Writers *For* Injustice?'

Dirk looked disconcerted for a moment, then shook his head. 'Sadly, you'd be surprised. But I wanted to talk to you about visas. Is this a good moment?'

Esko looked at his watch. 12.30. Then he glanced up towards Mariana and saw her shift her gaze hastily away. It was clear she had no idea how to handle the next few minutes, let alone the afternoon. Esko himself had made no plans. He had every intention of clearing his desk and showing up at a couple of random political meetings, killing the time until he and Amelie could meet up again the next day.

In the meantime some sort of peace needed to be made with Mariana. He turned back to Dirk.

'A very good moment, if you can bear to have lunch with me.'

Dirk beamed. 'Wonderful!'

'Fine, but first you must meet Mariana, my assistant. We'll bring her along. You'll get more sense out of her than me,' said Esko and guided his new guest over to where Mariana was doing her best to waste time re-ordering notes with paper clips.

~~~

A Simple Walk

Thursday lunchtime in Café Franck saw the putative commit-tee for the establishment of the Utterly Free University (UFU) in full session at the distant tables furthest from the door. A newly energised Elise, fresh from a morning of Modern Circus Studies, was holding forth – or at least was trying to whenever Kathrin was not (which was seldom). Hugo de Greef and Fidel sat on the leatherette banquette and eminence grised for all they were worth, largely silently. Catrina was in attendance, her new Plaid Cymru employer having disappeared back to Wales with the instruction that there was no point starting the job properly till after the weekend. There were other ad hoc members clustered about the periphery.

One very ad hoc arrival, who took up a good deal of that peripheral space, was Louise Camille. She had been gathered up, rather than knocked down this time, by Catrina and, after both had expressed their mortification over their first coming together in collision, had happily agreed to join the throng.

Absent, however, was Saskia. She had finished her work in Parliament as early as her member and decided to challenge her ban, determined that no Belgian barman should decide where and when she was allowed to drink.

Saskia had come into the café a few minutes later, seen Louise (supposedly her new lover) supping with the enemy and departed without a word – or indeed being spotted - in a regal Dutch huff. There would be trouble ahead and music to face, if she had her way.

Saskia was not one to hang around once a decision was made. She would head for another quarter all together: St. Gilles perhaps. An 81 tram would do but that would mean hanging around at the tram stop and Saskia was in a mood. It demanded the sacrifice of exercise. She crossed the square and began to tramp up the hill towards Avenue Louise. So now, she reflected bitterly, she had left one Louise sipping drinks in betrayal only to head for a street bearing the same name. No doubt something tiresome would have happened before she left it behind too.

As she climbed, Saskia glanced in at the windows. Had she been less cross she would have lingered at the shop selling bonsai trees and little statues of the Buddha in curiosity if not admiration.

A little further on, she gazed into the plush recesses of one of the smart restaurants that were starting to spill over from the wealthier districts on the other side of Avenue Louise. The high-backed chairs and pristine tablecloths spoke of soup plates for the main dishes, with the food stacked in piles instead of laid side by side for the diner to choose in which order to eat it. There were men and women in suits filling most of the table, though the men mostly made a small concession to the more Bohemian nature of Flagey by taking off their ties.

More out of habit than real interest Saskia studied the framed menu on the door post. It was lunchtime, she realised, which was of course why she had ventured into Café Franck in the first place. She was hungry.

Had her irritated reaction to seeing Louise sitting with that little English cow been more about hunger than serious jealousy, she wondered? There was only one way to test it, she decided, and that was to eat: not here though. She would abandon the idea of going all the way to St.Gilles, take a bus back towards Parliament from the top of the hill and see if there were more loyal and congenial friends eating out in Place Luxembourg.

The fastest way would have been to go back down the hill and pick up a different bus in the square but Saskia was not a woman for whom retreat, even in such a simple thing as getting to lunch quicker, was possible. She strode on up the hill, punishing herself further by ignoring the tram that stopped beside her half way up.

One more window caught her eye or at least, to be accurate, the picture filling it from the inside did. It showed a voluptuous nude in green and blue splashed with vivid scars of red – as though the artist had hurled a bucket of blood at his distinctly queasy model. At first Saskia was mildly revolted but then the combination of fury and eroticism in the picture began to intrigue her. She glanced up at the name of the gallery, Nikita's, and went in.

The example in the window, she soon found, was one of the milder of the artist's offerings. The name was just given as Duclos so it was impossible to tell whether the paintings were by a man or a woman, a point that was left deliberately unclear in the handout which Saskia picked up just inside the door.

Male or female, the artist was clearly as frustrated and angry as Saskia, given the way she/he wrapped figures in barbed wire, gripped their flesh in claws and dragged them by the hair across fields of stones. At the same time the models' faces were strangely serene in their ghastly colours, or expressionless, and Saskia suddenly realised the artist was painting the modern sado-masochistic equivalent of all those mediaeval and counter-reformation depictions of female saints, enduring unspeakable bodily pain while staring rapturously (or vacantly, depending on your attitude to religion) into the middle distance.

She became more fascinated as she strolled round the room but more uncomfortable too, disturbed to find she was responding to the pictures not so much in horror as excitement. What did this say about her? And what did it say too about her weekend with Louise? Saskia was not sure she wanted the answer.

At last she reached the desk at the back of the gallery. There were postcards of the work from the show on it and a book for writing comments. Nobody was sitting at it but the door behind was open and she could hear the sound of someone talking Spanish into a phone.

She bent to the task of writing her name, email address and to think of a remark that was direct, honest but perhaps did not quite reflect the confusion that the paintings had made her feel. French would be best for that, rather than the bald statements of her native Dutch.

She scribbled and once satisfied pulled herself upright. Mercedes stood behind the desk, smiling.

Saskia started to speak, thought better of it, and fled back into the street.

~~~

Parliamentary Lunch

Esko's lunch with Dirk van Abcoude of European Writers Against Injustice (EWAI) was going swimmingly well, at least on the part of two of the three at the table close to the window in the Members' Dining Room of the European Parliament. Being a Thursday, there was no great pressure on tables and the atmosphere in the room was relaxed now the main votes of the week were out of the way.

EWAI was one of those pressure groups it did no MEP any harm to be having lunch with and, given Esko's week of media notoriety, to be seen to have no hard feelings on the subject of free speech stood him in especially good stead. He made sure that he greeted warmly the few members of the parliamentary press fraternity who were also lunching as he strolled to the table.

Dirk was equally at ease. It was precisely becaue Esko had made the headlines that he wanted to lunch with him. Campaigns need to be visible and the new escort, in any sense, of a rising young film star was a godsend to anybody trying to bring the obscure issues that EWAI championed to wider notice.

For once Esko ordered some wine as they sat down: a slightly unseasonable Alsatian pinot noir that was a favourite in the EP's Strasbourg building but not exactly Brusselois – red and fruity but chilled. He felt he deserved it and, frankly, Mariana looked as if she badly needed it. She sat confused and morose, studying the menu with a concentration it did not merit, as Dirk made his pitch and Esko burbled politely.

'Our issue,' announced Dirk once food had been chosen and a decent couple of mouthfuls of red had entered the system, 'is that EU governments, especially the British and Dutch, treat writers and other artists from difficult countries as if they were just car workers looking for a job.'

'Unless they want political asylum, with all the appalling risks of penury and detention that brings, writers are regarded by immigration officers as vermin at best. Even if they let them in to speak at a festival or launch a book, the authorities can't wait to stick them on a plane the moment the gig is over. Now, if they were footballers, of course, they could have visas and work permits with barely a glance at the form – but writers with ideas and opinions? – scary!'

'What do you propose we do?' Esko asked, 'After all, visas sadly are still matters for Member States and they love pretending they have power – even if it is only the power to make everybody's life miserable for no good reason.'

Mariana looked up approvingly. It was the first hint of a thaw. Perhaps, with some suitably liberal political views, he could become something less of a cad in her eyes.

Dirk pondered. 'Well there are parliamentary resolutions, of course...'

'Pointless,' Esko waved the idea away. 'They just enrage national politicians with an inferiority complex.'

'What about an own initiative report. You could do that in committee.'

'I could but in reality that would disappear into the under-growth after a huge amount of work for Mariana.' He looked up and saw a hint of disappointment on his assistant's face. 'On the other hand', he began to retract, 'it is always a possi-bility to get the ball rolling. What do you think, Mariana?'

'It is always important to have the research behind any action,' she announced with a hint of twenty-something pomposity.

'Oh, definitely,' agreed Dirk, warming to her, 'and we could provide you with all – or at least most – of the facts and figures you need. Some excellent case studies too.'

'You could make it a joint report: the justice and the cul-tural committees, since you're on both,' suggested Mariana.

Esko sipped his wine. 'Not a bad idea – not bad at all –

that's if you don't mind all the work.'

'I would be happy,' she answered firmly. 'I've never been given a chance to do a report of my own. It would be very important for my CV.'

'Yes, of course. OK, I'll put in for it when I see the committee Presidents next week. But, Dirk, I'll need a good excuse. I want at least two good and urgent stories of how people have been treated badly in the last three months. Roughing up governments is always popular in here but if we are actually going to change anything we will need to prove it needs to be changed.'

'No problem,' Dirk nodded. 'There's...'

'Don't tell me now,' Esko stopped him. 'Mariana, dear, could you spend an hour or so with Dirk after lunch plotting it with him? Then perhaps we could catch up later.'

'All right,' she looked grateful as well as surprised at how deftly Esko had restored things to normal.

They turned their attention to the food as it arrived, served with the flourish that the waiters reserved for members who were in the national news. Esko's little flush of notoriety with Amelie had made him a celebrity in a place where most people mistook institutional importance for fame. No waiter could care less about the politics but the lover of a film star; he was worth knowing. Esko had the good sense to realise why he was being favoured and made a point of being particularly pleasant to those who served him. He knew they would be telling stories in the kitchen and that sooner rather than later these would be broadcast.

Mariana realised it too and her scowl returned. Her boss watched the clouds gather and filled her glass again. He suspected there might be tears to deal with once they got back to the office.

Esko was saved by a text. Just as he was finishing his excellent rare tuna nicoise a message came through telling him to get over to his party leader's room as soon as possible – like now. There was a crisis. What that was, he would learn once he got there.

'I'm sorry,' he said, looking up from the mobile screen, 'I'm going to have to go.' He showed the message to Mariana, who nodded – immediately relieved that the text wasn't from Amelie. 'Dirk, it has been a pleasure. I'll leave you in Mariana's hands for the afternoon.' He squeezed her shoulder as he stood. 'I'll see you later. We'll catch up over a drink, OK?'

~~~

Gallery Impressions

Catrina came out of Café Franck in the Flagey building after lunch and unwittingly followed in Saskia's footsteps up the hill along the tram route towards Avenue Louise. Like Saskia again she paused in front of the virulent painting in the window of Nikita's gallery and was intrigued enough to push the door open. This time, though, Mercedes was ready and poised behind her desk at the back of the room and smiled warmly as Catrina came in.

'Hello,' Catrina smiled back, 'I didn't know you worked here.'

'No?' Mercedes looked puzzled, 'but I told you I had a new job only last night, when we were at the bar.

Catrina remembered and had the tact to put her hand to her mouth in contrition. 'Oh, yes – I'm so sorry. Of course you did.'

'It doesn't matter.'

'No but I should have remembered. I think either Elise's big scene with Fidel or all those mojitos Patrice was mixing me must have blanked out the details.'

'Well, anyway – here I am.'

'Yes,' Catrina paused, not sure how to go on.

Mercedes helped her out. 'Take a look around. See what you think then maybe you could have a coffee with me here if it doesn't get too busy.

The smile returned to Catrina's face. 'Thanks. I will.'

Silence reigned, apart from the squeak of Catrina's flat shoes on the polished floorboards and the click of Mercedes' computer mouse.

The paintings disgusted and intrigued Catrina in almost equal measure. There was none of the homo-erotic charge that had fired up Saskia's excitement an hour or so earlier but the passion that infused every splash and brush stroke impressed her. She walked round for a serious five minutes before breaking off and coming over to the desk.

'Do you like them?' she asked Mercedes tentatively.

'Not a great deal,' the Spanish girl admitted. 'They are very strong but not easy to spend all day with.'

'Or live with. I can't see many people buying them to hang over the fireplace.'

'No, but I think Nikita is hoping that big galleries or companies might be interested.'

Catrina tried to imagine one of them hanging in a corridor of the European Parliament. Perhaps not. Such depictions of unrelieved female anguish might well sum up how many of the staff felt but would not find favour with the old boys who had a rather more paternal view. For most of them the pictures summed up how they probably suspected their wives and mistresses really saw them and their world. She doubted if they would want to be reminded quite so starkly.

'How long are these here for?'

Mercedes glanced at the flyer in front of her. In truth she had been so pleased to get the job she hadn't really thought about the beginnings and the ends of shows. She was relieved by the answer, though. 'Until the end of next week, it says.'

'Oh well,' Catrina smiled sympathetically, 'you should survive till then. What's next?'

This flustered Mercedes completely. She started to hunt around in the drawers of the desk, realising that it was exactly the sort of thing she should know and have to hand all the time. Thank heavens it was a friend who was asking, although maybe that was worse. Now her new friend would just think she was hopeless and sat about drinking coffee and painting her nails.

'It doesn't matter,' Catrina tried to be helpful, 'I can always look on the website.'

'No, no...' insisted Mercedes and just as she wondered what the no might lead to her hand settled on a pile of cards in the second drawer she had fumbled around in. She pulled a sample out and glanced at it.

With relief she handed it to Catrina. 'Here you are – Abstract Seascapes by Antoine van Heulen. I think this is an invitation to the vernissage – yes, it is. Tuesday after next. Wine from 6.30pm. You must come along.'

Catrina looked at her with a grin. 'Why not? I'd love to.'

'And you must bring Patrice.'

'If he's free,' Catrina grimaced. 'You know how it is there.'

'Sure. But if he's working we can all go down and drink with him afterwards.'

As Catrina folded the card and stowed it away in her bag

Mercedes said, 'So what are you going to do now? Did you come up here just to see the show?'

The Englishwoman shook her head. 'No, just passing. I told you I have got a new job too.'

'Yes, I remember. An Irish member of Parliament.'

'No, Welsh...' Mercedes waved the distinction away. It clearly meant nothing to her. Catrina began to realise she was going to have to earn her wages from now on. 'but she's really nice, my new boss – unlike the slob I was working for before – so I thought it's time I dressed the part; started to look a bit more serious.'

'Good idea.'

Fleetingly Catrina wondered whether the Spanishwoman was implying that she dressed badly. It was true, of course, but there was no need to rub it in. Then she decided it would be easier to take the remark at face value.

'So I'm going shopping.'

Mercedes looked envious. 'Great. You know it's a bit boring here but I have to stay. Would you come back and show me what you've bought, then we can have that coffee?'

'Deal.'

Catrina left the gallery and continued up the hill, turning right onto Avenue Louise when she reached the top. Then she realised that would just take her down to all the designer shops round Stephanie where she would not be able to afford anything. New job or not, she was not in that class of shopper. So she retraced her steps and walked across the avenue to the slightly smarter side of Ixelles where the clothes were priced for humans, not fantasy women.

She mooched, meandered, window shopped, fingered cloth, wondered whether her British size 8 to 10 would match anything she could fit into in Brussels, tried on ten outfits in four shops, and eventually emerged with something in black and a dark red cotton suit that she was frightened made her look forty-five. In trepidation, and with the promise of shopkeepers that she could always bring the clothes back and change them, she carried them back down the hill for Mercedes' opinion.

~~~

Late Lecture

Lunch and the discussions in Café Franck about the potential shape and philosophy (more the philosophy than the shape, it has to be said) of UFU (the Utterly Free University) dragged on until a time in the afternoon when all good Italians would have been deep into their siesta.

So it was that a buzzing on Fidel's phone preluded a distraught call from a departmental assistant reminding him that he should have been across town and delivering a seminar at his current institution of higher learning twenty minutes earlier.

As if by osmosis Elise heard her phone go a few seconds later, and with much the same message. She was meant to be delivering a tutorial paper to her class on 'Elemental Trapeze in Russian Circus' and clearly wasn't.

She gulped the last of her mint tea and scuttled out in panic. Luckily her destination was in a building only five minutes walk or, in her current state, two minutes run away. She was lithe and fit, had had the presence of mind to bring her paper with her to lunch, and was speaking in front of her class before her older lover had reached the Flagey bus stop.

Fidel was not one to scuttle or panic, let alone rush. He knew, after nearly thirty years of dealing with students, that most would be as late as him or, if not, were perfectly capable of entertaining themselves for an extra few minutes. The lecturer being late meant less words to listen to, less notes to take and more affairs (in both the general and particular senses) to arrange.

He supped his coffee, sipped his brandy, and gradually prepared himself to depart. The rest of the party – Hugo, Kathrin and various attendants – turned their attention to official business of their own or drifted back to work.

The seminar Fidel was to give – on 'Ghetto Mentality in Post War Banlieu Social Housing' was one that he had given so many times before that he could recite it without preparing more than his traditional first line. The gist of it and the reading list was anyway permanently up on the students' intranet. So Fidel's mind was free to wander where it would on the ten minute bus ride to his university.

It wandered first of all to Elise, marvelling at the transformation in Fidel's fortunes and self-esteem in the few days since she had come into his life. The solitary curmudgeon was not quite banished yet but he was certainly in sullen retreat. The Fidel that was emerging had something of the smile of the Sphinx, an enigmatic quietness that suggested that he had found the answer to many things in life and that, if one was prepared to wait, he would be prepared to hint where the answers might be found.

A rather less generous view might be that he looked like an elderly tomcat who had found an endless supply of cream.

There were those who were looking forward to the moment when he made himself thoroughly sick but Fidel was unaware of them. He was not a man who minded much what individuals thought of him at the worst of times. As long as his reputation held up, Fidel was comfortably satisfied with life and he thought it likely that the news of his liason with Elise would be doing his reputation no harm at all. A student she might have been but she was not his student, nor in his field or university. So reproach could not be hurled at him in any way except by those who automatically disapproved of any other scenario than boy meets girl at twenty and marries for life.

The bus drew up a few steps from the nondescript sixties building that housed the university's sociology department and, barely thinking, Fidel climbed the stairs to the first floor which held corridor after corridor of seminar rooms. The one he always used, had used for quarter of a century, was relatively straight-forward to find compared to some: turn left at the top of the stairs, through two sets of swing doors, turn left and third room on the left. Fidel prided himself that at no time did he ever have to tell a student to turn right.

As he passed other rooms he could hear the faint murmur of other lecturers going through their routines. He opened the door to his room and the twenty or so students who had bothered to wait ambled back from the windows and began to take their seats.

To Fidel's nose came the familiar smell of industrial floor cleaner and inadequately washed or badly perfumed youth that seemed to remain constant, whatever the decade.

He launched into his talk before he had reached the front of the room, beginning his address with the word 'and' as if his absence from the room had merely been a pause in the sentence. No apology for being late, no explanation, no waiting for students to open the notebooks (he had early on in the technology banned computers or recording devices as a matter of principle; which principle he wasn't quite sure but vaguely mentioned the thought that students remembered more when they had to write it down by hand and transfer notes later – it might even have been true but it annoyed the new generation, which was the main thing).

On burbled Fidel. The group either listened or gazed as their minds wandered, through the window or at each other's loved and loathed backs.

Half an hour slipped by and Fidel moved into the second half of his peroration. People stretched and shifted, dealt with stiff backs and aching writing wrists. Fidel had always maintained a rule for himself not to actually focus on the students individually, seeing them only as a group while he talked. No names, no faces, attractive or otherwise, no meeting of glances or responding to interest; maintain the fourth wall at all times.

For once he failed. His eye was caught by the extraordinary flowing, curly mass of black hair of a girl half way to the back of the room and he stumbled over his words. A second later he caught the knowing eye and cynical grin of the unshaven young man next to her.

Suddenly he was furious. He realised how much he hated the room, the students, the subject he was teaching.

Without finishing his sentence he marched from the room, turned right towards the lifts, pushed the button for the fifth floor. There he barged into the departmental secretary's office and strode to the startled woman's desk.

'Professor...' she began indignantly.

'I resign. With immediate effect. You will have my letter this evening.'

And he left.

~~~

Ruptures In Paradise

By mid-afternoon on Thursday all the protagonists that had gathered in Café Franck at Patrice's beck and call, or to discuss the UFU, had drifted off to work and shopping. They were replaced by those with nothing more pressing to do: foreigners between meetings, writers between pages, artists between brush strokes or pausing in the search for random objects to install. And students.

Among the students who were neither taking advantage of the free wi-fi to browse (research, they preferred to call it, they insisted), nor in a group recovering from the day's intellectual exertions, there were a pair in the middle of the room by the window whose intensity could be felt several feet away.

Flamand and Agnestina were having their first row. It was a very quiet row and it took the form of looking so intently and silently into each other's eyes that any casual observer would have mistaken the looks for those of love, not war. They were in truth both. Agnestina had accused Flamand of lying, which was both inaccurate and unfair.

The problem stemmed from the day before when Flamand, waiting for Agnestina to turn up, had had his view of the door obscured by the enormous Louise, and had bent over to pick up his pen at the exact moment that his lover had pushed her way through the curtains and into the room.

Flamand had, in turn, been equally screened from her sight by Louise and, to complete the fiasco, he had switched his phone off by mistake. When Agnestina rang to find out where he was, there was no answer. She had turned back through the door of the café just as he had sat upright with the retrieved pen. Outside the door, as she left him an enquiring voicemail, she had herself been obscured by the curtains when Flamand had looked for her. But neither of them knew this. As far as Agnestina was concerned he had not been there. As far as Flamand was concerned, neither had she while he had waited for one and a half hours.

There was only one way to break the deadlock.

In furious silence they both got up, approached the bar, and waited for Patrice to notice them.

This took quite some time as he was brewing three glasses of the hated mint tea, pouring a beer and assembling a couple of cocktails.

As they waited the two estranged lovers stared steadfastly at the back of the bar, determined not to acknowledge the other. Agnestina began to drum her fingers on the bar which, although an unconscious tick aimed at Flamand, if anyone, was a mistake around Patrice. A show of impatience was guaranteed to send him to the far end of the bar for the next order. Those who drummed could drum in vain, however pretty they were.

Out of the corner of his eye Patrice noticed the action and resolutely turned his back.

Eventually the second barman, Damien, appeared from the storage area at the back and, more impressed by Agnestina's hair than her fingers, took pity on her.

'Are you waiting?' Damien smiled at her. He was confused when Flamand replied instead.

'Yes but we want to talk to him.' Flamand pointed along the bar at Patrice.

Damien shrugged, 'if you say so,' stepped over to his colleague and murmured in his ear. Patrice shrugged in turn. Behind them Flamand and Agnestina resumed their vigil.

Patrice took great deliberation over two cappuccinos, giving the milk extra steam to froth, pouring and layering the foam into the coffee with the care of a restorer of ancient mosaics then, after laying them reverently on the bar, he contemplated the till as if trying to calculate the circumference of the earth.

Only once the coffee's purchaser had been asked if he liked the weather, wanted another speculos biscuit, had enough sugar and intended to have a nice day, did Patrice lend his disinterested attention to Agnestina.

'Mademoiselle,' he began, 'I can tell you do not play in the orchestra that performs here in Flagey.'

She looked suitably disconcerted. 'Why?'

'Because if you did you would know that it is in the concert hall that they store the percussion instruments, not on top of the bar.' He looked pointedly at her energetic fingers. 'And further, you would know that in this bar cellists get served a long time before percussionists.'

Agnestina frowned and looked down at her fingers as if they were independent entirely from the rest of her. 'Oh, sorry, I didn't...'

'No matter, you have said the right word. What can I get for you?'

'Nothing.'

It was Patrice's turn to look confused. 'Nothing?' He looked at Flamand who shook his head. 'Then why are you waiting at the bar?'

'You see, we are having a...' she turned to Flamand, 'a dispute.'

'A discussion,' Flamand insisted.

'About me?' Patrice raised an eyebrow.

'No, no,' Agnestina continued, 'about us.'

'And so where do I come in. I don't think I have had the pleasure...'

'You were here yesterday?'

'Yes.'

'Did you see me?' Flamand butted in.

Patrice thought. 'Possibly. Possibly not.'

'And me, but in the middle of the morning?' Agnestina pulled herself up straight and gave her most appealing pout.

'Same, I am desolated to say. Possibly, possibly not.'

'Oh,' the lovers deflated in unison.

'Was there a problem?'

'He says he was here, waiting for me.' Agnestina accused Flamand.

'And she says she looked for me here and I was not but I was,' he retorted.

Patrice regarded them for a minute, a grin spreading over his face. 'And now you are fighting. Do you know the exact time?'

'No,' admitted Flamand.

'Yes,' said Agnestina, 'eleven-thirty,' adding triumphantly, 'I was precisely on time.'

'So, we can settle it. Damien!' called Patrice. His colleague emerged again. 'Can you take over for a few minutes? My friends here have a little research to do in the office.'

'Sure.'

In Autumn

Patrice beckoned the pair to follow him through the door at the side of the bar into the back room.

VII

Still Thursday

Surveillance Confirms

Patrice led Flamand and Agnestina through the kitchen, quiet now after the lunchtime rush, to the back office of Café Franck. The room was empty. The day manager was on a break since there was no need to supervise and the food receipts had all been totted up and filed for ready for the final tally at the end of the night. In any case her shift would finish in two hours and then the night would be someone else's problem.

There were two desks in the office. One, where the manager had sat and counted, held a computer, two in-trays of neatly sorted paper, a muddle of lists – orders to be made, staff rotas to be organised – and a collection of tea glasses each with a cold remnant.

The second desk was backed by a bank of screens linked to the CCTV cameras that covered the café from every angle including, Flamand was rather shocked to see, the men's urinals. He would be rather more circumspect when he used them in future. On the table top piles of CDs surrounded a second computer and keyboard but Patrice ignored them, reaching instead into the top drawer and pulling out a memory stick. This he loaded into the computer, waited for a file directory to come up in the bottom right hand screen then asked again, 'Eleven-thirty, you said?'

Agnestina nodded, 'exactly.' Flamand hung back and shrugged.

Patrice found the time file and clicked. While seven of the eight screens continued to show the café in real time, the last one flickered and reformed the images into a collage from the day before. Patrice looked at the time record, entered 11.26, and clicked onto each camera in turn.

'Where were you sitting?' he asked Flamand.

'In the middle of the room, quite close to the bar.'

Patrice selected a camera that showed the central area and the corner door. As the image was enlarged Flamand's hair leapt into view from above, at a table one row in from the bar, facing the camera with his back to the main door.

'Well that proves something, at least,' Patrice said. Flamand held his hands out in a gesture of vindication.

'But,' began Agnestina.

'Let's just watch for a few minutes,' suggested Patrice.

They watched as, a few seconds later, the couple at the table next to him, closer to the bar, put on their coats and left.

At almost the same moment Flamand glanced around him,

moved swiftly and plonked himself at the new table but this time facing the door through which he expected Agnestina to enter. He reached back to grab the notebook and pen that he had been using across the aisle. As he did so the pen dropped to the floor. He bent down to pick it up, eyes still looking towards the café entrance but at that moment two things happened.

The curtain billowed and Agnestina came through them and Louise Camille, on her way out, blocked the view. Agnestina glanced around, failed to see Flamand (who was scrabbling after his pen on the floor) and tuned her back to look into the other wing of the room. Flamand, of course, was not there. Agnestina reached for her phone and went back through the curtains in front of Louise so that when Flamand sat up again all he saw was Louise's capacious back filling the doorway.

'Eh bien,' Patrice explained. 'Now we know and can be friends again, I think.'

Flamand smiled. Agnestina, though, stood stony faced gazing at the still image on the screen that Patrice had frozen.

For her things were not so simple. She could see that she was clearly in the wrong. She could have searched the café more carefully. She could have waited a few moments before she resorted to her phone and stomped off outside. She might have had the patience to realise that Flamand could have been hidden from view, could have been downstairs in the toilet. The time had been, she now saw, not 11.30 but 11.28. They had both been early but she had just assumed he should have been there first to meet her. Why? Wasn't that a deeply old fashioned and sexist assumption?

Agnestina was in the wrong and she hated being in the wrong, hated having nobody to shift the blame to. She tried to blame that fat woman for blocking her view but in her heart she realised it was hopelessly unfair. A second's patience would have solved the problem. If she had had the manners to wait while the older woman went out in front of her, Flamand would not have missed her. Agnestina's sense of childish pique was not helped by Flamand's clear reluctance either to blame her or mention any of her shortcomings. To him it was just one of those things, one of fate's little jokes at the expense of foolish humans.

Reluctantly she turned as Patrice pulled out the memory stick and switched the screen back to its real time surveillance. Without a word she strode back into the bar, making sure she barged Flamand's shoulder as she did so, then glared at him as it had been he who had struck her.

Flamand looked both hurt and bewildered but Patrice grinned and put his finger to his lips, taking Flamand by the shoulder to stop him following the his girl immediately.

'A moment, I think,' Patrice warned. 'She wants a fight and if you go out with her now she will have one.'

'But why should we fight?' asked Flamand in desperation.

'Because that way nothing will be her fault again. And then she will feel better but she will think worse of you. So, stay with me. We will go back to the bar.'

They did. Patrice slipped behind it and ceremoniously poured two Kir Royales. 'See if this helps,' he said and waved Flamand away as money was offered.

The young man gathered up the drinks and looked around him. Agnestina was nowhere to be seen. Surely she had not just stormed out?

Flamand carried the drinks round and leaned against the far end of the bar from where he could monitor every public door more easily, and waited.

~~~

Irish Solutions

When Fidel resigned his post as Professor of Applied Rhetoric in mid sentence and left the building early (having entered it late) the world, even the relatively restricted world of Belgian academia, did not end. For years he had assumed, either through a touch of vanity or as a way of forcing himself to carry on with his job, that it might and perhaps should. Neither was there a desperate hue and cry behind him of weeping students urging him to return, beseeching him because he had been the sole reason why they had signed up to the course. Nobody, it has to be admitted, other than the principals involved in the incident, noticed a thing.

For twenty minutes the students assumed that Fidel had suddenly been caught short and would be back to finish the sentence when he was in a state to do so. After all, he had started the lecture with the conjunction 'and'. It was only when one of them mentioned that the allotted time had expired five minutes before that they realised nothing more would happen. Even then nobody complained, or even commented much. They just drifted away.

Even in the departmental office Fidel's outburst was just considered a tantrum. He was not the first and would not be the last teacher to storm in and resign on the spot. Rather like policemen with reports of missing persons or cats, they tended to let matters ride for twenty-four hours before making enquiries.

In the case of Fidel the chances were that they would leave it until there was at least a weekend in between his non-appearances before they would bother to ring and ask if he was sick.

For Fidel himself the turmoil was a little greater. He had calmed down enough to stop shaking by the time he had reached the main entrance to the building but a combination of determination and mild shame stopped him retracing his steps. Most of all he did not want to see again the girl with the flashing black hair or her sniggering boyfriend, if that was what he was.

By the time Fidel had climbed onto a tram heading south the shock had all gone. It was replaced by a feeling close to bliss – as if the university building – no, the whole campus – had been lifted from his aching back. He did not climb on board the tram, he floated up onto it.

The 81 tram would take him all the way back up the hills and down to Flagey but Fidel realised, as he settled down and watched the dingy buildings slide past, that he wasn't ready for that yet – nor the bustle and cosmopolitan energy of Café Franck, nor the mess and isolation of his own flat. The adrenalin of his fury had subsided and the slump that followed inevitably had set in.

What did he want?

On its own that was too big a philosophical question for the tram. But even the question 'what did he want to drink and where?' seemed a tough examination. Fidel was not a serendipitous person. For once, though, instincts and the Fates would have to take charge.

The tram continued to climb and still instinct pulled him nowhere. The Fates seemed to be busy.

Fidel stared at red brick and grey stucco with blank disinterest. At the top of the hill, with the 81 stuck in traffic queuing to cross Avenue Louise and descend the other side, his mobile started chirruping. It was a ghastly noise but it had been the default setting when he had acquired the phone and no-one had explained to him how to change it, or even that he could.

He glanced at the screen. Elise. Still he answered with his usual suspicious hello as if the caller was bound to be an impostor or, worse, an official.

'Hi,' Elise responded cheerfully, 'have you finished?'

'Yes,' admitted Fidel, failing to admit that he had finished totally, not merely the afternoon's lecture.

'Ok – great. So have I. Where are you?'

'On the tram.'

'I can hear that but where?'

'Louise.'

'Get out. I'll join you – but not in Café Franck. I don't want to go back there now.'

'Neither do I,' Fidel said with relief.

'Fine. There's an Irish pub on the corner by your stop. I'll be there in ten minutes.'

'But...' But it was too late. Elise had rung off before Fidel had time to say that he hated Irish pubs unless they were in Ireland, where they were sensibly called bars as they should have been in Brussels.

He didn't feel like ringing back and organising something else, though, and in any case this might not have been the moment for cultural semantics.

The tram lurched forward across the junction and Fidel made his way to the door without enthusiasm. He turned back to the corner and glanced up at the sign before he climbed the steps of the pub. The name had changed, he felt certain. He couldn't quite remember what it had been before (named after someone political, perhaps?) but he was sure it had not been O'Driscoll's.

It was early enough, that time when the borders of afternoon are confused with evening, for the bar to be quiet and the free tables to be plentiful. Fidel sat down at one with a view of the door and waited. He was waiting for Elise, of course, but he was also waiting to be served. Nothing happened. The bar staff glanced at him occasionally but made no move to come out from behind their barricade.

A few minutes later, as promised, Elise ran up the steps and bustled over to him.

'What's the matter? Don't you want a drink?

'Of course but no-one has come to serve me.'

'Darling,' Elise infused the word with a killer dose of tolerant exasperation, 'it's the same as Café Franck. You have to go and ask at the bar. Nobody comes to you.'

Fidel sniffed. 'Ah.'

'It doesn't matter. I'll get them. A beer?'

Fidel shook his head. 'No – and especially not one of those glasses of black mud they call beer.'

Elise waited patiently. Eventually Fidel made up his mind. 'Maybe I will have one of their whiskies with a lot of ice.' He fished a twenty euro note out of his pocket. 'I have something to tell you. You may need a strong drink too,'

When she returned with the drinks – identical choices in the end – she was frowning. 'What is it?' she asked with a hint of trepidation.

Fidel took a swig. 'I resigned. In the middle of my lecture.'

'Instantly?'

'Yes.'

Elise's reaction was not what her lover had expected. She beamed at him. 'Oh, that's so good. Now you will be completely free - to build our own university!'

~~~

Complicated Dressing

Catrina had been shopping. She had also promised Mercedes, holed up in Nikita's contemporary art gallery where she had just started as the assistant, that the results of the expedition would be brought back for approbation or disapproval. Catrina, being Catrina, was convinced as soon as she left the door of the boutique clutching her suit bag, that disapproval would triumph.

Mercedes was elegant and Spanish. Catrina, in her own

reckoning, was a nondescript little frump from Derby.

The feeling that her purchases were an inevitable disaster grew with every stride down the hill from Avenue Louise towards Place Flagey and by the time she reached the gallery's door she was in such a funk of shy inadequacy, she almost walked straight past. But she didn't quite.

She hovered, slowed, glanced in the window and so could not ignore the beaming smile and cheery wave that Mercedes sent her from the back of the room. Catrina smiled unconvincingly back, stopped and dutifully pushed open the door.

'So you bought something, I see.'

'Yes,' admitted Catrina, 'but I'm not sure I like it now – and I'm sure you won't.'

'Oh don't be silly,' Mercedes brushed away the thought, 'come through to the office and try them on for me.'

'You mean it?'

'I insist. You never know,' she said, taking Catrina by the arm and steering her to the back of the gallery, 'if I really like them I may just tell you they'd look so much better on me and steal them.'

The office was a light airy room with desks against two walls, a large rack for pictures taking up most of the space, and a tall window overlooking gardens at the back. Mercedes chattered as she went to close the blinds.

'I won't leave you in the dark but we don't want the neighbours getting excited as you change, do we? Where did you go? Surely not down to those Paris chains at Stephanie or that dreadful galleria?

'No – too much money there, I'm afraid.'

'And the things are all so badly made. The clothes may have the right labels on but you know they've been stitched in a sweat shop in Bangladesh and will fall apart on the third wearing. Of course, most of the women who buy in those shops never get that far. Twice on the body and then into recycling or off to charity.'

Catrina drew the little black dress and the red suit from the bag and laid them out on the nearest desk. 'Which do you want to see first?'

'Oh they look so good, I can tell already,' enthused Mercedes and Catrina felt some of her shame ebbing, though she was still convinced that once she was wearing the clothes she would ruin their line anyway. 'I think I want to see the red.'

Catrina kicked off her shoes and shuffled out of her jeans and jumper. Now it was not just the new clothes she was worried about but her undistinguished underwear: plain beige bra and unshapely black and white striped knickers bought in multi-packs of ten.

Mercedes, she was sure, would be all in red or black lace if undressed. In this she was right (it was all black that day) and indeed the Spanish women did think that Catrina's Englishness showed up more glaringly in her drab smalls than anywhere else but Mercedes was much too sensitive to say anything.

Instead she waited as Catrina slipped on the red skirt and helped her with the zip and hook at the back, then stepped away as the jacket was added. Catrina ran hands through her hair so that it fell free across the collar.

Mercedes was all encouragement. 'Oh my dear, you're transformed. So smart!'

Catrina could have taken this to mean she usually looked a mess but decided for once to be positive. 'You like it?'

'It's delightful on you,' Mercedes confirmed. 'Go to the end of the room and walk back – wait, no,' she opened the door to the gallery, 'let's give you some space. Walk from the front.'

This was, Catrina felt, making her a little bit more of an exhibition than she had intended, especially as a full tram stopped just outside at that moment, but the whole point of buying a bright red suit was to look good in public so she'd have to brave it sometime.

Mercedes watched her saunter down the gallery, turn behind the big canvas in the window and come back. She clapped. 'I was going to say you looked more like a Member of Parliament than they do but it's much better than that. You shine!'

A new wave of doubt hit Catrina. 'Do you think it's too much? I mean, will it look as if I think I'm trying to upstage my new boss?'

'No, she'll just be impressed that you mean business.'

'Well, if you say so.'

'I do.' Mercedes gave Catrina a little push back into the office. 'Now let's see the other one.'

Catrina was more confident in the neat black dress, tight around the body but loose enough in skirt to flow, with the hem a respectable but not spinsterly couple of inches above the knee. She changed and repeated her modelling routine across the floor of the gallery to a similar torrent of approval from Mercedes (with the slight reservation that 'you'll need a different bra, a little less padding I think', which just touched another of Catrina's insecurities).

All in all, though, she could count her rare afternoon in clothes shops a moderate success.

The door was closed behind Mercedes, allowing Catrina to change back into her street clothes in peace. She had just stripped off the dress when she heard the bell of the gallery's street door tinkle to announce a visitor and heard Mercedes' guarded 'hello'. She bent over to pick up her jeans from the floor. It could hardly have been a less dignified position so when the office door was thrown open she was not even able to see who it was that exclaimed, 'Well now. Look at that! Mercedes?'

It was a deep voice but, despite Catrina's confusion, she registered enough to thank heavens that it seemed to be female.

~~~

Peace Is Harder Than War

Flamand sat at the end of the bar, back to the toilets, in Café Franck and surveyed the crowd, inside and out. Agnestina was nowhere to be seen. She was clearly taking the hump elsewhere. Even at his tender age Flamand had discovered enough about women to know that it would have been much easier if he had been genuinely in the wrong about their failed meeting of the day before. He would have been punished, of course, but after looking suitably crestfallen for a bit, he would have been forgiven for a price.

As it was, Agnestina had been at fault and he had to wait before she had dealt with her own fury before she was likely to want peace with him. So, at Patrice's suggestion, he watched the bubbles evaporate from the glasses of Kir Royale and bided his time.

He wondered if he should order himself a drink in the meantime, the cocktails being their joint offerings to Agnestina, but decided rightly that to be caught would render the gesture empty. He watched and waited.

Outside Agnestina paced a circuit of the building. She wanted the confusion and the crossness to fade away but neither were obliging. Why were men so insensitive – or rather, when men were being sensitive, why were they so annoying anyway?

A cigarette (she didn't really smoke, honestly) was found and lit. She had almost completed her way round the block when she realised that would bring her into view from the bar's windows. She turned and walked back the way she had come, waiting for the nicotine to work its magic.

Halfway round calm gradually returned. Agnestina stopped and watched a pigeon risking its life in the traffic for a morsel of bread.

There was a choice to be made. She could just go home, texting some excuse to Flamand, but that would be the end of the affair in every sense.

Flamand would probably weep, shrug and forgive her anyway. That wasn't the point. The point was that she wouldn't be able to carry on – her irritation at his unwarranted forgiveness preventing her from finding him interesting any more.

Or she could nonchalently amble back into the bar, return to Flamand (it never occurred to her that he might have left too), smile sweetly and wait for him to apologise. Apologies could only come from him. For her to offer them was inconceivable, especially when they were deserved.

Outside the Flagey Centre's box office she paused, drew on the last of her cigarette, and dithered. It came down to a simple decision. Was she ready to ditch Flamand or not? Had she exhausted her fascination with him? Her conscious mind didn't really know. She let the part of the brain that controlled her feet take charge.

Even then not much happened. The feet took her in circles. Lighting a second cigarette – a signal of true stress – Agnestina reviewed Flamand's pros and cons. There was the way he flicked his hair across, definitely a con. There was his adoration; a con when he went all droopy about the eyes but a pro in that Agnestina quite liked being adored as long as it didn't lapse into total wimpishness. His prettiness helped, though that too might pall. Not yet, though.

Resolution struck and Agnestina trod her half smoked fag underfoot and strode back into the bar.

Flamand, who had been on the point of giving up and going home, beamed as he spotted his girl re-enter. As she found him and came over to join him he said nothing but just pushed the glass of kir and champagne in her direction. She nodded, kissed him softly on the lips, and sipped the proffered cocktail.

At the other end of the bar Patrice spotted the reunion and grinned. His analysis and his solution had both proved spot on.

He was still grinning when Catrina appeared in front of him laden with bags, the fruits of her shopping trip and consultation with Mercedes. She interpreted his smile as all for her and Patrice was feeling sufficiently pleased with himself that he saw no reason to explain anything different. Instead he came round the end of the bar and enveloped his English lover in a hug.

'Thanks,' she said, 'I really needed that.'

'I am happy to hear it,' he acknowledged, then took her by the shoulders and looked carefully at Catrina's face. 'But why? Has something happened? The shopping was bad?'

Catrina grimaced. 'The shopping was fine but afterwards... Get me a gin and tonic fast and I'll tell you about it.'

Patrice obliged, helped himself to some water and, nodding to the other barman to hold the fort for a few minutes, ushered Catrina over to the customary table at the end of the counter.

'So?'

'So I bought the new dresses...'

'Can I see them?'

'Later. And you know Mercedes, who I spilled that tea over?' Patrice nodded. 'Well, you know she has a job now in a gallery up the street and when I looked in she made me promise to bring the clothes back and try them on; to see if she approved, I suppose.'

'That's kind.'

'Yes, and I did because, though I was worried what she would think, I did promise.'

'And did she approve?' Patrice asked.

'Oh yes, but then it got ridiculous. I was just stripped off, changing back into these things, bending over to pick up my jeans, when her boss – that Russian woman – walked in on me.'

'Emabarrassing.'

'Totally. So bad. And she made it worse.'

'She didn't scream?'

'No. She said – "my dear, what an installation. Stay just like that – in those cotton things. I must have you projected on the back wall for the winter show". Catrina gulped her gin as Patrice guffawed. 'I know it's funny.'

'I'm sorry, it is.'

'But it's worse. She meant it. I've spent the last half hour explaining that I couldn't possibly.'

Patrice leaned across and kissed her. 'No my cherie – not for her. But for me, always.'

~~~

Political Crisis

In response to the texted summons, Esko left Mariana and the man from the European Writers Against Injustice organisation at his lunch table in the European Parliament's Members Dining Room, paid the bill on the way out, and made his way up the towers. When he reached the spacious office of Roberto Vincenzi, leader of the Social, Liberal, Enterprise and Ecology

(SLEE) group to which they both belonged, he found a grim-faced bunch perched around the desks and sofa.

He smiled and nodded a greeting, found a door jam to lean against, and waited to be told what was going on.

There were six men and two women filling the rest of the room, not counting Roberto and himself. All were MEPs and he noticed that there were no assistants in attendance. Since the whole group only consisted of thirty it was a fair proportion of the possible attendees. More would have demanded a proper meeting room and Esko could see by the faces that something confidential was in order.

The unsmiling nods he received in return were confirmation that bad news was coming too. He wondered if it could be for him. Had his public snog with Amelie Poitiers been too much for the pursed-lipped keepers of Parliamentary morals? He doubted it. There were plenty of members with unconventional personal lives, including Roberto, and anyway, that call for personal freedom in the face of conservative community disapproval was meant to be what the party stood for.

'Ah, Esko, good that you could make it,' Roberto did not sound as if he entirely meant anything of the sort.

'No problem. How can I help?'

'That we shall see. You've heard then.' Roberto's voice was full of quiet distress.

'Heard what?'

'So you have not. We are in a little difficulty, I am afraid.'

Esko adopted a suitably serious expression and waited for

enlightenment. Most people seemed to be examining their fingernails or the ceiling. He waited ten seconds then asked, 'Any one want to tell me about it?'

Roberto waved his hand defensively. 'It is of a fiscal nature', he offered by way of explanation, then lapsed back into silence.

The wait resumed.

Eventually an exasperated voice broke the deadlock.

'Ja, so somebody must tell you so I will.' Esko looked across at the woman with short dyed blonde hair, glasses and leather trousers resting on the arm of the grey sofa: Brigitte Etzenberger, from the Ruhr bit of Germany. He nodded his thanks.

'So Roberto is being accused of false expenses, not here but before, when he was a member just of the Parliament in Italy.'

'I thought it was virtually impossible to think of anything that could not be expenses in Italy,' suggested Esko unhelpfully.

Roberto sighed. 'In the old days....' his shrug left the thought open.

'The problem is not the accusation,' Brigitte continued, 'it's the amount and the attitude of the prosecutors in Rome. They allege €680,000 over ten years, and they have applied for a European arrest warrant. Roberto has immunity while he is a member here, of course, but there is pressure on us from the proctors and the other groups to waive it, for the good name of the Parliament.'

Esko frowned appropriately. 'Yes, I see. That is difficult. Roberto, can they make a good case?'

'In Rome anybody in politics can be given a sting. My enemies sting me. Whether or not I have given myself a little help with cashflow now and again, it will take years to prove either way.'

Esko found himself feeling very northern European. 'Sure but will we look stupid if we defend you?'

Roberto's shrug almost lifted his whole body from the chair. 'How can I say? What is stupid these days?'

Very quietly Esko said, 'Stupid is when we say something that is clearly rubbish in the face of the facts – or when we look to the outside world as if our party name, SLEE, really is short for sleaze, as all the cartoonists and bloggers suggest. And this week I am an expert on cartoonists and blogggers.'

'But your career and freedom are not in danger,' said Roberto.

'My career could have been. Luckily the press like my little love excursion and realise that my about to be ex-wife has been just as active in Helsinki.'

'Ja, well, that is not for now,' said Brigitte firmly – everything was said firmly by Brigitte, 'but this is clear. We do not have to throw Roberto to the dogs but group leader he cannot be. He will get all the fire and the media will talk of nothing else, not even Esko's sex life.'

Around the room there were murmurings of agreement. Even Roberto nodded forlornly. 'I think I will have to step aside, as they say. But I will not renounce my seat; not until I am sure I can win the battle in Rome.'

From next to Esko the sphinx-like eyes of Luxembourger Jens Sauer opened half way. 'Then who will step in for Roberto?'

The silence returned. They all knew that the Luxembourg compromise was the one they especially wanted to avoid but with Jens standing there they could hardly say so.

'It's not just us in here,' Esko pointed out. 'There are thirty of us with a vote, so there is time for people to put themselves forward.' Nobody seemed eager to agree or disagree.

Once again Brigitte took charge. 'Ja, well now I should tell you that we have been meeting before you and Jens arrived from your lunches and we have decided to elect you, Esko.'

'Me? Why?' Esko looked appalled. 'And what about the rest of the party?'

Brigitte waved the question aside like a wasp. 'They will agree. Sheep always do. You want to know why? It is precisely because of the way you have handled the last week. The media love you, the public know who you are. Also you are honest and your votes show you believe in what we do.'

All this was said to Esko but most eyes were on Roberto who hung his head.

'And what if I don't like it?' asked Esko.

'You will,' Brigitte announced.

~ ~ ~

No Time For Contemplation

'Give me an hour', said Esko – if he had to take the position of Leader then he at least wanted time to adjust his thoughts to the prospect. If he was sure he wanted to refuse then he needed time to make that argument too. 'There are people I should talk to.'

Once again the Germanwoman took charge. 'No, Esko, all the people you need to talk to are here and we have told you what we think. We cannot wait around and neither can you. Either you want to lead us or you don't – and we want someone who can take a decision, not a 'one hand – other hand' character. It is not an offer that will come again.'

She was right, he realised. Esko gazed out of the window across the city of Brussels for a minute, then circled the faces around him. Jens, Luxembourg's hope, was staring at the floor, clearly miffed that he had been ignored and excluded, and Roberto was fiddling with a pen, already half withdrawn from his political life. But otherwise the faces were excited and expectant.

'Yes then,' Esko heard himself say. Then his conscious

mind caught up. 'You will still give me an hour though. And we will do this properly. Roberto, you will call a meeting of the whole group for 1600. There you will resign but you will insist that we cannot leave the room without a new leader. In the meantime each of you will talk to two other colleagues and see that I have a willing majority. If not I will insist the meeting has a debate whatever you have decided in this office. I will not try to lead a party that is divided from the beginning.'

'But Esko...' Brigitte began.

'No, Brigitte, you want a decisive leader, now you have to live with it. So, if there is clear backing for me I will do it. I will need to be proposed formally for the ballot. Jens, if you are happy to do that then it will prevent many bad moments in the future.'

The Luxembourger looked first startled and the sheepish. 'Me! Why?'

'You know as well as I do. I don't have to spell it out here.'

The two men locked eyes then Jens smiled, 'OK, that will work.'

'Thank you. I think so too. Brigitte, you will second me. It is better that way round, don't you think?'

'Ja, if you say so,' but there was a hint of disappointment. She had wanted to carry the role she had taken in their caucus onto a wider stage.

'Now let's save anything else that you want to say till later. I need to make some calls. Roberto, I will stay here just until your assistant can check that our usual meeting room is free.

It should be on a Thursday.'

After the other members had filed out, Esko sat down heavily on the couch and grimaced at the man who was about to become his predecessor as leader of SLEE. 'I didn't imagine this ever happening, let alone want it, you know.'

Roberto smiled grimly. 'It was not a turn of events I anticipated either. Politics! I am sorry. I have enjoyed being leader. But not any longer, I think. With these accusations the fun will soon disappear so you are welcome to have a little time in the line of fire.'

'That's kind of you. Why me, though?'

'You heard the German. She is right. That should be good enough,' Roberto thought for a moment, then said, 'My old mentor explained something to me when I was becoming a candidate for the first time. He said, "politics is not about great plans; it is about great management of the unexpected which makes everyone think you had great plans". That is what we have a chance to show now.'

~~~

French Backing

Back in his own office Esko was relieved to find that Mariana was still out – whether extending her lunch with Dirk or just doing her own thing he really didn't care. He closed the door to her part of the suite and slumped into the chair behind his desk. Hell, he thought. This was not going to be easy.

His mobile buzzed with a text message. He glanced at it and grimaced. Amelie, just wondering how his day was going. He was about to call her back when the thought of film stars phones being hacked made him pause. Instead he texted back, 'Fine. Any chance you can come EP right away? I'll explain...'

The answer was a relief. 'Twenty minutes.'

Again, the unexpected. He would have Amelie in the room with him if and when he was elected. It would mean Amelie and Mariana would have to meet too. Better now than later; no point in giving his lovelorn assistant time to build up her distress. Esko leaned back in his chair and closed his eyes. Amelie was the only person he had needed to call, really. His wife Rikka could find out from the media – there was no need to forearm her. That left his parents and brother but it would be better just to tell them the result if he was elected.

Esko was waiting just inside the public entrance in good time to fetch Amelie and texted Mariana to be waiting in the office when he returned. Amelie swept up the steps from her taxi and into his arms. 'This is a surprise,' she said after the kiss.

'I know. There is a bigger one coming. How do you feel about being a political girl-friend?'

'Seriously?'

'Seriously.' Esko bent to whisper into her ear. 'There's been a sudden revolution in my party's group here in Parliament. They want me take over as leader – and they want you too.'

'OK – I think,' said Amelie cautiously.

They joined a short queue to the reception desk so that she could be signed in for a visitor's pass. The middle aged man taking the details took her passport, looked at the name, looked up at her face and blushed intensely before busying himself with the details at twice the normal speed, even standing and bowing when he handed over the badge. Amelie gave him her sweetest smile and he nearly missed his chair as he tried to sit down again.

'That's why,' said Esko. They made their way to the lifts and paused as he took Amelie to one side. 'I want you to be in the room for the debate and the election. It will make it clear that if they want me, they get you too. If they don't, that's their business and nothing changes for us either way. And now you have to meet my assistant Marianna. I think she may cry a little.'

Amelie shrugged. 'That's show business,' she said but inside she was wondering whether she could stand any more situations laced with vinegar in one week. 'What are your politics, by the way?' she asked as they waited for the lift doors to open.

'Nothing too embarrassing. Sometimes they condescendingly call us the gentle left.' Esko smiled and squeezed her arm. 'You never know, you might even find you agree with me.'

'Nonsense darling,' teased Amelie, and returned the leer from a plump lobbyist across the lift with a pout full of impossible promise.

VIII

Second Saturday

A Peaceful Weekend?

On Saturday morning, the first after Catrina's incident with Saskia's mint tea over Mercedes that had resulted in so much more than a hot wet shirt, the Café Franck was busy by eleven. The weather outside had turned viciously autumnal. Rain swept the length of the lake and splattered against the windows. Underneath tarpaulins the steel chairs fended off rust. Inside, the radiators gurgled into action for the first time since April.

Catrina had arrived earlier than she would usually have, partly because Patrice had been at work since eight, partly because the alternative was taking the dirty washing to the grubby launderette up the street and she needed coffee and conversation before she faced that. There was no reason to get in Patrice's way, though. She was happy to plonk herself in a distant corner and read the newspapers from home online.

Occasionally her lover broke away from the counter to become her personal barrista and sneak a quick kiss. That was enough to keep the morning sweet.

A few minutes later Mariana pushed the curtain aside and came in. Catrina spotted her, frowned, and shrank back against the wall out of the Finn's line of sight. Their last encounter in the Parliament had not been happy and Catrina had a feeling that Mariana's humourless intensity was unlikely to keep her Saturday morning relaxed.

Had Mariana seen Catrina she would have ignored her too; the last thing she needed was the Englishwoman's attempts at cheery tact.

It was a black morning for Mariana and she had dressed for it: black jeans, shapeless black jumper and heavy coat. She bought a double espresso black coffee and headed for a two seat table close to the radiator with her back to the door. She thought it unlikely that Esko and Amelie would be heading in somewhere so public this early in the day but if they did, she wanted to be in a position to ignore them as well.

At the table next to her, facing in the opposite direction, sat Fidel, absently tearing a croissant to flakey shreds. He had come to realise that any interruption to Elise's life before it was absolutely necessary in the morning would be at best unre-warding, at worst painful. He had resumed his old routine of pushing some cold water over his face and hair, throwing some clothes on and heading out for his wake-up coffee, picking up a paper at the Moroccan newsagents on the way.

Normally he reckoned to have finished his second coffee and be on to the first beer of the day, having reached the racing pages of the paper, before Elise would poke her head somnolently through the curtain. This routine had in fact only been running for half a week (and that broken by tumultuous events) but already Fidel could feel the subtle shift in that comforting word, normal.

The café was filling up steadily, faster than usual because the chill rain made sitting outside untenable. Those looking up to greet friends often found that all there was in front of them was a curtain billowed by the teasing wind.

Saskia, stubborn Dutch to the core (or perhaps from the core), had decided to ignore Patrice's ban from the previous Saturday. She was lucky that he was out of sight when she arrived at the bar and that the girl serving her had no inkling of the old drama.

With bull-headed cheek Saskia selected exactly the same table as she had occupied a week earlier. Had she been challenged on the omens for this she would have said that it was not the table that had caused the problem but the inattentiveness of an Englishwoman who had all the dreary characteristics of her race; hiding deviousness behind an air of vague civility.

The only one of those descriptive words Catrina, sitting five yards behind her, would have accepted was 'vague'. For the rest she would have said it was typical of such a hard nosed bitch to judge by her own intolerant standards.

Patrice, happening to catch them both in view as he returned to his post and his professional eye swept the room, wondered with amused anticipation whether another collision between them might enliven this Saturday. Better not to chance it, he decided. He was not going to create a scene by actually going to Saskia's table and forcing her to leave but she would not get served again. He gathered his colleagues together and gave the judgement.

As so often in the previous fortnight, Mariana's assessment of Esko's actions turned out to be wrong. He and Amelie had decided there was no point in holing up all day in either her hotel room or his flat (they had spent the night in the latter). In any case the damp and cold had confirmed the paparazzi and gossip reporters' view that the story was unlikely to have any new angles for the moment and only a hardy and otherwise unemployed pair had staked the door from early morning.

Esko and Amelie felt they should return to the building of their first meeting and judge whether their notoriety would make a public breakfast too much of a trial by staring. As they strolled over the film star, professionalism switched on, made a point of posing for the damp photographer and offering the reporter the sweetest of platitudes in her most confidential purr.

In the event the most they faced was a slightly dumbstruck couple at the bar, who ceded their right to be served first, and an unnecessarily obsequious filling of their order for café complet by Patrice's fellow barman, Damien.

Amelie thanked all three with a disarming smile, creating fans for life just as she had of the photographer and journalist standing by the lake in the rain a few minutes before. The new celebrities then carried their breakfasts along to the table next to Catrina, Patrice departing from his usual aloofness by taking charge of their orange juice.

Catrina carried on reading The Guardian on her laptop. Though she knew Mariana from Parliament she didn't recognise Esko again and had been far too absorbed in her own affairs (in every sense) to have noticed Amelie and hers after the quick glance at lunch on Tuesday.

She saw Patrice place the orange juice with care and smiled up at him as he returned to the bar.

Mercedes and Louise entered at the same time, ordered and went their separate ways Louise saw Saskia, wondered whether to join her and (once spotted) realised she could hardly do otherwise without causing offence.

Close by the window facing the lake Flamand and Agnestina had settled down together. There had been a moment during the week when that had been no foregone conclusion. As it was their relationship had shifted, imperceptibly to each other but subtly to themselves. Agnestina was still without parallel in Flamand's experience or affections but her fit of pique a few days earlier had made him aware that he was going to have his hands full. She was no longer perfect.

For her part Agnestina knew she had been a bit of a cow but had decided that Flamand would do as her first term lover, though love was too strong a word as yet. She felt more like a cat being stroked: pleasant enough until something more enticing came along.

~~~

Clothes Lines

There was a lull in the morning's rush to the counter and Patrice had a moment or two to rest his hands and survey the room. As he caught the backs or faces of customers he knew, he reflected that a lot had happened in such a short time. People had fallen in and out of love. Some had found jobs, others lost them. Celebrities had been revealed, nonentities were still nonentities.

About Flamand and his gorgeous girlfriend he was not sure. He detected a hint of reserve where before there was only reservation. The thought made him glance across at Catrina. A few days earlier it had been Patrice himself who was feeling that reservation was the best policy. Now he was certain, as certain as a barman who spent his life flirting with available women could ever be, that he had embarked on a different voyage from his usual inconsequential affair. Maybe. Who could tell?

His reverie broke and he switched the smile back on as coffee was demanded. There had also been the tap of impatient fingers on the bar. Normally such a tap would have resulted in instant reprimand or at least the order being ignored for a pointed five minutes. Patrice did not like being tapped at. House rule. He glanced to see who the perpetrator was, ready for a tussle.

He relented almost immediately. Instead of the moronic middle-aged man he had expected he was greeted by the grinning face of Nikita, her blonde hair piled impossibly on top of her head in the way that only Russian women still seemed to think suited them.

'So Cherie, you were dreaming, I think. I hope it was a happy vision?', the gallery owner ventured.

'It was,' Patrice admitted.

'You had the look of a man in love.'

'Maybe, you never know.'

'That is truer than the young ever realise. While you are deciding you can, please, make me a machiato. It will interrupt your dream for less time than a cappuccino. Ah, my dear, good morning.' This last greeting was to Mercedes who had just appeared at her elbow. 'I was just explaining that I would not keep our friend from his dreams too long. But what will you have? We will make him delay again.'

'An espresso. Grand,' Mercedes requested, slightly mysti-fied. Patrice, his back already turned as he snapped the coffee filter into place above the cups, nodded.

As he turned back and laid the full cups on the counter he said, 'and if I was dreaming it is possibly your fault, at least a little.'

'You're not in love with me, are you?' Mercedes was cross to feel herself blushing.

Patrice was gallant. 'Sadly, no – not for the moment any-way. I was thinking that if I had only had to wipe mint tea off the floor a week ago, instead of from your shoulder, I would not have met Catrina and Catrina is...'

'Special?'

'It seems so.'

'Do I know this paragon?' asked Nikita.

Patrice pointed with his head. 'She's over there.'

Nikita followed his sign. 'Oh her! Last time I saw her she was nearly naked.'

'I'll explain later,' Mercedes stepped in and ushered the Russian away from the dumbfounded Patrice before he remembered the story Catrina had told him on Thursday afternoon.

They looked around for a free table but, approaching the middle of a damp Saturday, Café Franck was yielding none. The only chairs free were at Catrina's so, hoping that Nikita would behave herself, Mercedes led the way up the step.

Catrina's brow was furrowed as she read the online Guardian's account of the UK's latest devolution arguments, an issue that she would have barely considered a few days earlier but, now that she was about to be assistant to a Plaid Cymru MEP, realised she had better get her head around.

'May we?'

Catrina looked up, startled. She saw Mercedes, smiled, then saw Nikita and was instantly flustered.

Nikita did nothing to help. 'I was just telling that sweet man who is, I believe, in love with you that the last time I saw you, you were wearing almost nothing. It seemed to surprise him.'

There was nothing really that Catrina, in her English disarray, could say. She and Mercedes blushed together. The odd thing was that Nikita did not seem to be trying to be either facetious or smutty – just amused.

Eventually Catrina recovered her tongue. 'I can't imagine why,' she said. 'He saw me in less this morning.'

From the next able there was a snort and then a fit of giggles. Catrina turned to see a supremely pretty woman reaching desperately for a glass of orange juice and a Nordic man smiling in mild embarrassment.

'I'm sorry,' the woman said, 'it's that you have just summed up my week perfectly.'

'And you explained it beautifully on television just now,' said Nikita without turning a hair as she recognised Amelie. 'I watched you just before I came out.'

'Thank you.'

Recognition began to dawn on Mercedes too. 'Oh, you're...'

Catrina looked at the faces in utter bafflement. One minute she had been reading a serious article in The Guardian about Welsh politics and the next she was in the middle of a multi-national discussion on nudity. Esko came to the rescue.

'Hi,' he said, 'I'm Esko – you work in the Parliament I think. I've meet you with my assistant Mariana.'

'Right,' muttered Catrina, gradually finding herself on firmer ground.

'And I'm Amelie Poitiers.'

'Of course you are dear,' announced Nikita grandly. 'We all know that.'

'I'm afraid I don't,' admitted Catrina. 'Should I?'

It was Nikita's turn to be amazed. Mercedes just smiled, torn between delight at meeting Amelie and new found admiration for Catrina at standing her ground.

'No reason at all,' charmed Amelie. 'In fact it's wonderful to meet someone who doesn't. I'm an actress and so the papers here like taking pictures, especially with Esko.'

'How annoying,' said Catrina, imagining herself in that position. 'I'm sorry, I've had a week when I've only been reading the English ones and I don't think you've been in them.'

'Then, perhaps, we should spend the rest of the weekend

in London,' Amelie took Esko's hand.

'Not a bad idea,' said the Finn.

~~~

Train Plans

While Esko and Amelie were making instant travel plans to cross the Channel for the afternoon, on the other side of the room Elise was just cradling her first coffee of the morning and wrenching her mind into a condition to allow her to talk. Fidel waited patiently, reading his newspaper folded on the table in front of him and sipping a beer.

The week had been momentous for both of them and they were glad to slip into Saturday with nothing planned or anticipated, letting their minds take bearings without that word used so much in Saturday sports commentary, 'pressure'. Fidel himself never looked at the sports pages, except to look for contemporary material for his sociology lectures. Had she been asked Elise would have admitted to a sneaking admiration for a few of the world's tennis players but little of that was due to the intricacies of the sport itself.

Nobody, least of all Fidel, was going to ask Elise anything until the coffee was lodged in her system, though.

In truth both felt they had done enough talking that week. There was a great deal to assimilate before any more steps were taken. This morning was for joining each other in companionship that had nothing to do with passion but everything to do with understanding and the emergence of affection.

Their silence was nothing compared to, indeed wholly different from, the chilly one that enveloped the table over Fidel's shoulder. Saskia was glaring at Louise with a frigidity that could have reduced the North Sea to icebergs in a day. Louise had no idea why. She had smiled, carried her own coffee across, kissed her lover of last weekend affectionately on the cheek, and settled down to catch-up on the gossip.

Saskia had shrugged and turned on the frozen Dutch indifference. Which would be worse, she wondered; to start a conversation and be ignored or to wait in tense anticipation until Saskia decided to say something?

At her side, at the window table, Mariana looked up and fumed with misery. It was simply not fair. Not only had she been wrong to think that Esko and Amelie would not show up, they were now in happy discussion with that little bitch Catrina who, she suddenly noticed, seemed to be a special pet of the good-looking barman.

A week earlier everything in Mariana's life had been just fine, or at least not actively malignant. She was doing a job she loved for a man she loved in a city that felt chic and sometimes even exciting. So much had gone sour. It was as if the very building was mocking her; the café with its jolly music, the couples comfortable in that late morning lazy quiet and easy communion requiring no active conversation.

As so often, Mariana's reading of people was more self-conscious assumption than accurate insight.

Flamand and his beautiful Agnestina were engaged, not in the transfer of mutual understanding but in wary introspection that was about halfway between Elise's hungover blankness and Saskia's deliberate cold shoulder. There was love of a kind but it was going to need a fire lighter to get it going again.

Esko, ever the efficient organiser, was looking up train times and hotels for the London escape on his phone screen. They had just missed one train, he discovered, and would have to wait a surprising three hours before the next one. Rooms in London were no problem for the weekend but the price of both was eye-watering. And he was travelling with a film star so first class was essential. He wondered if he dared put it on parliamentary expenses and let the thought perish quickly. That way, these days, lay real political ruin as it had so recently for his erstwhile party leader, Roberto.

Nikita and Amelie were striking up an instant friendship, at least that was how Nikita saw it. While they did so, Esko did the gentlemanly thing and booked the travel. His little revenge on distant Finland and Rikka, his about-to-be-ex-wife, was to use the credit card attached to their joint account. Their combined salaries could easily stand the strain but still he looked forward to the expletives Rikka would erupt with when she opened her next statement. He wouldn't be anywhere near, of course, but that didn't lessen the anticipated pleasure. It was extraordinary how their feelings had changed in a week – or maybe it was just his that had changed. Rikka's were already on the wane.

Time to switch his own salary out of that account, he thought. Revenge was likely to be two-sided.

'But my dear!' Nikita was exclaiming, 'I think you would love my gallery. The artists I have are just like the parts you play. Passion, beauty, the chance of tragedy.'

Amelie murmured politely. 'Thank you.'

A gleam came into the Russian's eye. She looked immediately conspiratorial as the brainwave hit her. 'It's perfect!' she announced with the finality of a woman who is never contradicted. 'Of course, you must be our Patron. No duties, just your name and you and your charming man must come to as many parties as you can. You epitomise everything I want the gallery to represent – youth, fashion, excitement, integrity...'

'Well,' Amelie baulked at the gush of flattery.

'Now don't resist. You will have a ball.' Nikita looked at Esko, Catrina and Mercedes for support. 'Won't she?'

They all smiled but knew better than to interrupt.

'I won't be able to come to every opening,' warned Amelie, 'there is filming that makes planning so hard and, you know, I live in Paris, not Brussels – at least I think I do.' Esko grinned and kissed her hand.

'Luckily I can get a train in that direction too,' he said.

Nikita's brainwaves were getting overheated. 'And you know I've always wanted to have a gallery in Paris. I will start looking and in the Spring you will open it. That's settled.'

Amelie could sense defeat. She nodded and muttered, 'Why not?'

Across the floor, where Saskia faced Louise, Mariana moped and Agnestina toyed with Flamand, Patrice could see trouble brewing.

He looked at his watch. Midday. End of shift. The troubles of customers were no longer his. He shed his apron and slipped into the seat next to Catrina. It was time for better things.

Till Next Time

Autors Note

The idea for writing a series of pieces set in a Brussels café lurked in my mind for almost twenty years. I had watched the way the European Parliament had become part of Brussels' intellectual and artistic life, turning a rather self-absorbed Belgian capital into a cosmopolitan melting pot as it drew in young assistants from all over the continent. At first I was tempted to concentrate the stories in Place Luxembourg or the Parliament itself but then I found myself hanging around the Café Belgo (renamed the Franck here) on the corner of the concert hall and arts centre in Place Flagey. The area is a wonderful amalgam of all the contradictions that make the city so extraordinary at the start of the 21st century.

I owe thanks to Kate Milsom, for her wonderful illustrations, and to Eugenia Lyras who contributed cartoons to the original blog posts. Thanks as well to Kathrin Deventer and Hugo de Greef, who have allowed me to turn them into fiction, and to Alexander McCall Smith, who suggested that I could write episodes not for a newspaper (like his Scotland Street series for The Scotsman) but as an internet blog. Unlike him, I have nowhere near the discipline to post an episode every few days. The intention was to make it weekly on the Hay Press site but even that never quite happened and the 50 episodes here stretched over two years. With luck I will manage the next 50, for *Flagey In Spring*, in rather better time.

Also available from Hay Press

SIMON
MUNDY
Silent
Movements

Silent Movements

The last years of the Soviet regime. Being a great violinist or a young composer could make you a state asset or a target. When Alexander Kryzhinski finds that his lover Elena is being persecuted he knows it's time to defect. Who to tell and how to do it is more dangerous.

In the early 1980s Anthony Westfalen is a British cellist just beginning to make a name for himself. He finds, though, that international politics is never far from the music business and playing a concerto is just the start of it.

Simon Mundy's novel accurately recreates the tension that gripped the final cold war period and the way it intruded into the comfortable world of classical music.

'Simon Mundy really knows the point where music, politics and history collide. He also understands the processes of a performer's life.'
Julian Lloyd Webber

£7.99

Simon Mundy
By Fax To Alice Springs

By Fax To Alice Springs

By Fax To Alice Springs was Simon Mundy's second book of poems, including work from 1987 to 1995. As the title implies, the poems were written all over the world – North Carolina to Italy, Moravia to Australia – as well as in Mundy's home territory on the borders of Wales. They reflect his intense sense of the spirit of place as well as his wry approach to politics and bittersweet relationship with women.

'Mundy can be cheeky, he can be rueful but he is always passionate.'
Daljit Nagra

£8.50

Published by Gwaithel & Gilwern the poetry imprint of Hay Press.

Poem from *By Fax To Alice Springs*

Jazz Brusselois

In this dank little Brussels square
Backed against the traffic, careless
Of the festive music, such as it was
(Only a Belgian could think the organ
A proper instrument for jazz)

A woman stood behind a tree
Her come-on shoulders twitching to the rag,
Attached to no-one, wore no rings,
Should have washed her earth brown hair
To spare our imagination, the lonely men

Who edge up close, trepidated,
Weighed a starting speech so not to frighten,
Could fall in context, bring out a shallow answer
To release her conversation, our convivial
Gratitude and a proffered round of drinks

From the owner of the café on the corner
Who shared our persistent admiration.
Even walking to the car
Smiling a chaste kiss-on-either-cheek
Continental-way goodnight

Even in the caught-you-at-work
Caught-you-at-home, dull supper
Sleepless night calls
That followed for a month or two
I could never have guessed that once we kissed

Excavated deep over dinner (of course
Belgian women prize their food above
Their lovers), compared our lives
Rehearsed the past, the only legacy would be
The boredom, the relief that she ordered
The taxi to drive on and leave me
Silent at the door.

HAY
PRESS

Hay Press is a general publishers based in the
Hay-on-Wye area of the Welsh Marches.

For other titles available including the novels,
Seeking the Spoils, *Shadows On The Island*
and *Counter Coup*, see our website
www.haypress.co.uk.

Follow us on Facebook
facebook.com/haypressbooks
and Twitter
twitter.com/haypressbooks